THE SECRET OF
THE LOST AMULET

THE SECRET OF
THE LOST AMULET

BY VALENTINE J. BRKICH

ISBN-13: 978-0-9816877-8-0

Bridge Street Books
P.O. Box 84
Beaver, PA 15009

Illustrations and cover design: Zach Schaffer, zachschafferart.com
Interior layout: Cassie M. Brkich, BrkichDesign.com

For Isaac and Antonella

1.

"All right, everyone. Let's call to order the weekly meeting of the McIntosh History Hunters Club."

Nellie rolled her eyes. "You know, Logan, you don't have to be so formal about it. I mean, it's just you, me, and Bubba. Geez."

"If you don't mind, Nellie, as president of the club, I prefer to run things in a proper manner. Now, if you will please light the ceremonial candle, we can officially begin the meeting."

"Yes, sir, Mr. President," replied Nellie, offering a sarcastic salute. Striking a match, she lit the candle that sat on the large stone in the middle of the room. Although she thought Logan had a tendency to take things a little too seriously, she did enjoy this particular aspect of the club's standard procedure. Something about the light flickering from the candle and bouncing off the cave's cold, damp walls inspired her. It seemed to connect them to the past and put them in the right state of mind.

Of course, Logan had a unique ability for putting a damper on the mood. "For today's meeting," he began, "I'd like to discuss Fort Brodhead."

"Ugh," said Bubba, sporting his usual backwards trucker cap and chewing on a Popsicle stick. "Can't we talk about something else? *Anything else?* I mean, c'mon, we've talked about the boring old fort like a gazillion times. I'm sick of it."

"Yeah, me too," added Nellie. "It's been done to death. Besides, it's not like anything cool ever happened there."

Logan crossed his arms in disgust. "What's wrong with you guys? Are we a history club or aren't we? History-wise, Fort Brodhead's the biggest thing that's ever happened to this town. Heck, there wouldn't even be a town of McIntosh if it weren't for the fort!"

The Fort Brodhead site was on the other side of town, near the river. Built by the Colonial Army during the Revolutionary War, it was meant to serve as a base of supply for the army in its maneuvers throughout the frontier. After the treaty with the local tribes was signed in 1785, the fort was decommissioned and gradually picked apart by settlers moving into the area to start a new life. The only remnant of it now was a lonely monument that few, if any, townsfolk ever paid attention to.

Bubba leaned back on his rock and stared up at the cave's stone ceiling. Nellie just sighed and rested her chin on her hand.

"And 'nothing ever happened there'?" Logan continued, doing air quotes. "Are you kidding me, Nellie? Ever hear of the—"

"The Fort Brodhead Treaty," Nellie broke in. "Yeah, yeah, yeah. Everybody knows about that. Who cares? Just another boring treaty, if you ask me."

"Yeah, and another *boring* treaty that the Colonials just ended up breaking, just like all the rest," added Bubba.

"Exactly, Bubba." Nellie stood up and paced around the cave. "I just wish something a little more exciting had happened there. A battle, a siege—anything!"

Logan frowned. "Well, I'm sorry that our town's greatest treasure is so boring to you two. But there's nothing we can do about that." Logan turned on his iPad and pulled up his information on the fort. "Now, I'm the president of this club—"

"For now," Bubba interjected.

Logan glared at him. "*And as president,* I get to choose the first subject of the meeting. And I choose Fort Brodhead."

Nellie huffed. *Oh, well,* she thought. *It's not like we have a whole lot to talk about anyway.*

"Now," Logan began, adjusting his always-too-short necktie, "can either of you name the first and last commanding officers of the fort?"

Just as Nellie and Bubba began to ponder Logan's question, a silhouette temporarily blocked the light from the cave's entrance and Johnny came stumbling in, looking as frazzled and disheveled as ever.

"Hey, you guys!" he said, gasping for air. "Did you hear...the big news?! I can't believe it! They're comin' here! Here! To McIntosh!"

Logan frowned again. "Well, lookie who's here. And right on time as usual, I see. Meetings start at three o'clock sharp, Johnny."

"Yeah, yeah, I know," Johnny replied, still trying to catch his breath. "But this is big. I mean REAL big! It's the biggest thing that's ever—"

"Well, are you going to tell us what it is or aren't ya?" said Bubba, still chomping on the Popsicle stick.

"*History Hunters* is coming to town! The TV show! They're coming here to film an episode! Isn't that cool!?"

Nellie couldn't believe her ears. *History Hunters* had been her favorite TV show for as long as she could remember. They even named their own club after it. Johnny was right. This was huge! Not that she was about to show her excitement. "Oh, yeah? That's cool," she said, taking a seat on her rock. "Although, they'll probably just wanna do some dumb show on the fort or something."

"Dumb? That would be wonderful! Finally our fort would get the kind of recognition it deserves," said Logan, looking over at Bubba and Nellie. "No matter what *you two* think."

Bubba stuck his tongue out in reply as Logan returned the gesture.

"Personally, I don't care why they're coming,"

said Johnny. "I just think it'll be cool seeing the town on TV. Hey! Maybe I'll get to be on TV too! Whoa..."

"Oh, boy," Bubba replied, "now *that* would really bring the ratings down."

Johnny took a seat around the candle with the others. "Ha-ha, Bubba. Very funny. But, hey, it could happen. Seriously. Heck, I might even get to meet Rick Jenson himself."

Nellie sat up on her rock. "Rick Jenson? He's coming here?"

"Well, yeah," said Johnny, quickly passing his hand back and forth through the candle flame. "I mean, he is the show's host and everything. And here's the coolest part: he's coming to the high school tomorrow for a press conference! At least that's what I heard. Tomorrow afternoon in the gymnasium. Whole town'll be there, I bet."

"Wow!" said Nellie. "Rick Jenson...here in our town!" She leaned back against the damp wall of the cave, smiling as she pictured the charming host in her mind, with his perfect hair and million-dollar smile.

Bubba elbowed Johnny and gestured toward Nellie. "Maybe you can give him a big fat kiss on the lips, Nellie," he said, making a silly looking kissie face that drew a good laugh from the other two boys.

Nellie's face turned visibly red, even in the low light of the candle-lit cave.

"I don't know why you even like that show in the first place," Bubba added. "It's not like they ever find what they're looking for."

Bubba had a point about that. They never did seem to find anything. But Nellie didn't care. History was her passion. It was one of the reasons she loved this cave so much. According to legend it was an old haunt of the Delaware tribe, the Leni Lenape, who used to inhabit the area around McIntosh. It was so cool to think that early Native Americans might have taken shelter or performed ancient ceremonies right here in this very cave. It was really the only reason she'd agreed to make it their official meeting place, despite her fear of bats and creepy-crawlies.

"Well, I'm going no matter what," said Johnny. "I mean, this is—"

"Big," said Logan. "Yes, Johnny, you already said that. And I'm sure we all plan on being there. As the town's only official history club, I'd say it's our duty to be there. But for now, let's get back to the subject at hand—Fort Brodhead."

As Logan reiterated the history of the fort, which they had all committed to memory by that point, Nellie sat back and thought about tomorrow when, hopefully, she'd get to meet her hero—Rick Jenson.

2.

The next day was Sunday, and after the morning church services the auditorium at McIntosh High was packed to the gills. Johnny was right, it seemed like the whole town was there. On top of that, there were at least two local TV news crews, as well as a reporter and photographer from *The Quay County Tribune*—the town's on-line newspaper.

Bubba, Logan, and Johnny managed to grab three seats way in the back. Nellie, however, had stood in line for hours and landed a primo seat, dead center in the third row, where she waited anxiously for the arrival of Rick Jenson.

Finally, at one o'clock sharp, Principal Anderson stepped out onto the stage and approached the mic. "Good afternoon, everyone! And welcome to McIntosh High! This is a very exciting day, both for our school and for the town of McIntosh."

Nellie was literally sitting on the edge of her seat, craning her neck to try to see over the heads of the writers and TV reporters in front of her.

"So," continued Principal Anderson, "who here is a fan of *History Hunters?*" The crowd erupted in applause. Way in the back, Bubba and Johnny let out a loud "Woot! Woot!" while Logan rolled his eyes and politely clapped.

Principal Anderson was practically giddy. "Well, then," he said, "have we got a treat for you! Ladies and gentlemen, it is my great pleasure and honor to introduce to you the host of *History Hunters*—Mr. Rick Jenson!"

Nellie sat up straight in her seat, beaming. Once again the crowd broke into applause as the handsome television host walked out onto the stage.

Rick Jenson had it all. He was tall, good looking, and charismatic. On top of all that, he was the host of the most popular show on the History Channel. As he strutted out on stage, Rick waved to the crowd, his pearly white teeth twinkling in the bright auditorium lights. Nellie was beyond excited. She couldn't believe it. Here he was—Rick Jenson—right in front of her! It was the first time she had ever seen an honest-to-goodness celebrity in the flesh. And he was even more handsome in person—not that she really cared about that kind of thing.

Rick stepped up to the mic, bowed, and mouthed the words "thank you" as he motioned with his hands for the crowd to take their seats. "Thank you! Thank you all! And good afternoon, McIntosh!"

As the people continued to cheer and clap, Bubba turned to Johnny and said, "Geez, you'd think it was the president of the United States or something."

Finally the crowd fell silent. "Wow," said Rick, "what a warm and inviting welcome! Thank you. On behalf of the entire *History Hunters* team and crew, we are very excited to be here in your charming little town. Thank you for this amazing turnout."

Nellie stared up adoringly at her idol. She was beside herself with excitement. Meanwhile, down in front, photographers flashed away, trying to get the perfect shot.

Rick continued. "McIntosh, as you all know, is a town rich in history. Fort Brodhead, for example, played an important role not just in the founding of this town but also in the history of our great nation."

Nellie sighed. *Oh well,* she thought. *At least our town will be on TV, even if all they care about is that boring old fort.*

"Now," said Rick, "I'm sure most of you think that Fort Brodhead is the reason we're here today. Well...it's not."

Nellie sat up in her seat as mumbling erupted throughout the auditorium. *Not the fort?* she thought. *Then what the heck are they here for?*

A sly smile grew across Rick's face as he spoke into the mic. "Let me ask you this: how many of you have ever heard of the Native American Chief Pisquetomen?"

"Pis-keh-what?" said Bubba, turning to Logan and Johnny, both of whom just shrugged their shoulders.

Down in front, Nellie was thinking the same thing as she turned to look at the many confused faces around her.

"No one?" said Rick, clearly pleased that

he had stumped the crowd. That is, until he saw one solitary hand pop up way in the back by the door. It was the hand of Nellie's seventh-grade-history teacher, Mr. Vincent. "Ah!" said Rick. "Looks like we have a winner. You, sir, in the back...what can you tell us about the great Chief Pisquetomen?"

One of the *History Hunters* crew made her way over to the teacher and held out a microphone.

"Well," Mr. Vincent began, "he was a leader of the Turkey Clan of the Delaware people who originally emigrated to and inhabited this region back in the early to mid-18th century."

Rick seemed impressed. "Very good, sir. Anything else?"

Mr. Vincent continued. "Yes. As a young man, he was contracted by the English to be a guide and interpreter during the French and Indian War."

Nellie and the boys were stunned. Mr. Vincent had never mentioned this Pis-keh-whatever person in any of their classes.

"Again, my compliments, sir," replied Rick. "It looks like we've found McIntosh's preeminent history buff."

Mr. Vincent politely smiled at the few hundred

faces that had all turned around to look at him.

"But what you probably didn't know, Mr. History Buff, is that, in addition to Pisquetomen's valuable leadership skills, legend has it that he also possessed magical powers—powers that enabled him to appear and disappear at will and travel great distances in the blink of an eye!"

From the look on Mr. Vincent's face, you could tell that he did, in fact, know about these so-called magical powers. But the person with the mic had already walked away.

"And," continued Rick, "that these magical powers were supposedly due to something the great chief wore around his neck."

The boys turned and looked over at their teacher, who looked back at them, smiled, and mouthed the word "amulet."

"An amulet!" echoed Rick. "A green emerald amulet, in fact, which Pisquetomen was said to have worn at all times. Though its existence has never actually been verified."

Nellie sat captivated.

"Now you're probably wondering what happened to Pisquetomen and his magical amulet," said Rick. "Well, unfortunately, no one knows for sure. That's why we've come to your enchanting little hamlet—to see if we can finally put an end to this mystery. Being of great value, the amulet—if it ever really existed at all—was most likely spirited away by someone upon the great chief's death. That said, we have reason to believe that Pisquetomen himself—well, at least what remains of him—is still somewhere right here in the town of McIntosh!"

Once again the auditorium was filled with excited mumbling from the crowd. By this point even Bubba was literally perched on the edge of his seat.

"And…" Rick added, waiting for the crowd to quiet down, "…and, in the coming week or so, we hope to gather some information that might give us a better idea of the location of his final resting place. And when we do finally locate and confirm the identity of his remains, the great Pisquetomen will finally be memorialized in proper fashion, and deservedly so."

And with that Rick Jenson left the stage to a standing ovation from the jam-packed auditorium.

Nellie couldn't believe her ears. Native American chiefs! Magical stones! This was better than she could have ever imagined. She turned around in her seat and looked to the back of the theater where the boys were sitting, beaming as she made eye contact with them. Settling back in her seat, she began to imagine the great chief and his magical amulet walking along the riverbank back when the town was nothing but a vast forest of towering trees. *Wow,* she thought. *This is so cool. How'd I never hear of this Pis-keh-whatever before?*

Immediately after the press conference, Nellie made her way through the crowd, hoping to talk to Mr. Vincent, but he was busy giving an interview to the reporter from the *Trib*. So instead she went off to see if she could find Rick Jenson and maybe get his autograph.

Down by the band room, Nellie found a large crowd of people standing around. "What's everybody waiting for?" she asked a security guard standing nearby.

"They're all waiting for Mr. Jenson," he replied. "Autograph seekers, I guess. Not sure if he's coming out or not, though."

Nellie nodded and quietly snuck away from

the crowd. From her time in the middle-school play, she knew about the back entrance to the band room, so she decided to see if she could get a sneak peek at her favorite TV host. Quietly pushing on the back door, she nudged it open just far enough so she could see Rick sitting on a couch and talking on his cell.

"Who cares if I mentioned the amulet?" Nellie heard him say into his phone. He looked visibly agitated as he took a sip of bottled water. "And no one here has ever even heard of the guy. Well, except for some old fart in the back of the auditorium. Look, don't worry about it. They'll never know if we find it anyway."

Nellie was shocked. Old fart? Was he talking about Mr. Vincent? Who was he talking to anyway, and why were they talking about the amulet?

"Besides," Rick continued, "we had to mention the stone to see if any of the local yokels might have any information on it. Our incompetent researchers couldn't dig up much on it. And the last thing I want to do is spend a week in this dumpy old town just to find out that what we were looking for is already sitting in some local museum."

Dumpy old town? Nellie couldn't believe what she was hearing.

"Look, you just leave everything to me, OK? Have I ever let you down before? Right. I'll call you as soon as I have any information." And with that Rick hung up his phone.

Just then someone poked their head in through the main doorway. "Excuse me, Mr. Jenson, but they're waiting for you."

"Yeah, yeah," replied Rick, taking another swig of water. "Let 'em wait. I'll be out when I'm good and ready." Then, mumbling under his breath, "I don't know why I have to waste my time talking with these morons."

Just then Rick started talking to someone else in the room who Nellie couldn't see. "You have one week," he said. "Don't let me down."

"Don't worry," came a raspy reply. "I won't."

And with that Rick stood up and stepped out into the hallway, where he was greeted by more cheers and applause.

Suddenly the door Nellie was spying through swung open and a man stepped out. Luckily Nellie was shielded by the door and he didn't notice her. She didn't get a clear look at him but could see that he had longish black hair and a scruffy, unshaven face. She sat quietly until the man disappeared out a side exit.

Nellie sat back against the hallway wall, stunned. Rick Jenson certainly wasn't the same person he pretended to be on TV. Worse yet, if she had heard him correctly, it seemed like *History Hunters'* main objective wasn't Pisquetomen after all—they were after the amulet!

3.

That evening Nellie decided to do a little re-search on Pisquetomen to see what, if anything, she could learn about the old chief. Unfortunate-ly, her search was coming up empty.

"This is crazy," she said, staring at her laptop screen. "How can there not be anything about this guy anywhere?"

Next she Googled "amulet":

am·u·let
noun am·u·let \ ˈam-yə-lət \

Def: a charm often inscribed with a magic incanta-tion or symbol to aid the wearer or protect against evil (such as disease or witchcraft)

"Whoa! Cool." Maybe the internet couldn't tell her about Pis-keh...whatever, but Nellie knew who could: Mr. Vincent. And she was going to find out everything she could.

The next morning when the kids arrived at school, they all made a beeline for Mr. Vincent's room. Nellie, a star on the middle-school cross-country team, got there first.

"Well, good morning, Nellie!" said Mr. Vincent, as she came crashing into the room. "I'm glad to see you're so excited to get to class. But you know, history isn't until after lunch."

Nellie was in no mood to kid around. "Mr. Vincent," she began, trying to catch her breath, "how come you never told us about this Pis-keh...Pis-keh..."

"Pis-KEH-toe-men," Mr. Vincent replied, slowly enunciating the syllables.

"Yeah," said Nellie. "That guy. How come you never told us anything about him?"

"Well...you never asked."

"Seriously, Mr. V!"

Just then Johnny and Bubba tried to enter the room at the same time and got stuck in the doorway.

"Johnny, you idiot!"

"Hey, I was here first, Bubba!"

The two boys were suddenly dislodged from the doorway as Logan gave them a hefty push from behind. "There," he said, sauntering into the room. "You two cretins need to learn how to properly use a door."

"All right, boys," said the teacher. "That's enough. I suppose you're all here for the same thing?"

"Yeah, Mr. V," said Bubba, popping a fresh Popsicle stick in his mouth. "So what can you tell us about that old Indian dude Rick was talking about yesterday?"

"Native American, Bubba."

"Oh, yeah. Sorry, Mr. V. *Native American* dude."

Nellie and the boys took a seat and listened intently as Mr. Vincent told them everything he knew about the great Delaware chief. About how he had emigrated to this area as colonists began to encroach on his people's tribal lands back east. About how, as a young tribesman, Pisquetomen was wary of serving as a translator and guide for the British, but felt it was the best thing to do for his people. About how he turned against his British allies after they failed to follow through with their promise to leave the tribal lands. And about how he mysteriously vanished from history sometime around 1760, along with his so-called magic amulet.

"So nobody knows what happened to him?" asked Johnny. "Just—POOF!—and he was gone?"

"Not exactly," said Mr. Vincent. "Some people think he went further west. Others say he died from smallpox. And some even speculate that he was *murdered*."

Nellie's eyes widened. "Murdered? By who?"

"Yeah, and why?" added Bubba.

"Well," said Mr. Vincent, "by us."

Logan sat up in his seat. "What do you mean, by us?"

"The Americans, of course. You see, kids, when the Revolution broke out and the Colonial Army built Fort Brodhead here along the river, there were still a few Indians living in the area."

"Native Americans, Mr. V."

"Touché, Bubba. Excuse *me*—Native Americans." Mr. Vincent continued. "Anyway, one of these was an elderly Delaware chief they referred to as Old White Eye. Now you see, Old White Eye served as a go-between with the

Americans at the fort and the remaining tribes-people in town, helping with things like trade, disputes, and whatnot.

"Well, when Old White Eye died sometime around 1780, reportedly of smallpox, he was buried somewhere right outside the fort. His people, however, wanted the body exhumed so that they could give it a proper ceremony on sacred ground. But the Americans refused their request."

"But that doesn't make any sense," said Nellie. "Why would the Americans care where he was buried?"

Bubba agreed. "Yeah. And what does this have to do with the murder of Pisquetomen?"

Mr. Vincent smiled. "Actually, it has everything to do with it, Bubba. You see, some people—and I'm one of them—believe that Old White Eye and Pisquetomen were one in the same."

The kids' mouths all dropped open.

"Wait...what?" said Logan. "I thought you said Pisquetomen died twenty years earlier in 1760?"

"Actually, Logan, I said that he *disappeared* around 1760. In all my research, I've never found anything about his death. I did, however, find something interesting about his appearance."

"OK," said Bubba. "So what was it?"

"Apparently, Pisquetomen had one white eye, most likely the result of a cataract."

"Whoa!" said the boys in unison.

"Whoa is right," replied Mr. Vincent. "A lot of times in history, especially this era of history, when so little was actually written down, stories and people can get misconstrued. Hence, the confusion with Pisquetomen and Old White Eye."

"So, if Old White Eye really was Pisquetomen," said Nellie, "then that means he could still be buried right here—in McIntosh!"

Mr. Vincent nodded. "That's correct. And apparently the *History Hunters* folks have come to the same conclusion."

"Wait a minute," said Johnny. "Hold everything. Let's say this Old White Eye dude really was Pisquetomen and he really is buried near the fort site. That still doesn't explain why they wouldn't let his relatives dig up the body and take him home."

"That's precisely why many people think it was murder," replied Mr. Vincent. "If it really was disease that killed him, the Americans wouldn't have cared if his tribe members exhumed the body. Then again, if there was a wound, say from a musket shot...well then, that would be an entirely different story altogether."

"I don't get it," said Logan. "Why would anyone want to murder him? Wasn't he on the Americans' side?"

"Well, Logan, one reason could have been that he was becoming—pardon my French—a real pain in the butt. Pisquetomen made it known that he would only pledge his people's assistance to the Americans during the war as long as the Americans agreed to hit the road once the war was over. And being so highly respected by his people, he could end up causing the Americans a lot of headaches if he wanted to. That, or maybe, just maybe, someone was after his so-called magical amulet."

The children sat quietly as they let Mr. Vincent's words sink in. Could it really be true? Was this great Delaware chief, and possibly his magical amulet, still buried not far from where they were standing? It was like something out of a movie.

"OK, Mr. V," said Bubba, "if Pisquetomen really is—"

But just then the bell rang to signal the start of the school day. "Look, kids, we can chat about this some other time. Right now you better hurry off to class."

As the kids all headed out into the hallway and toward their homerooms, Nellie's head was spinning. Could Mr. Vincent be right? Was Pisquetomen actually murdered and buried right here in McIntosh? And if so, did that mean the amulet might actually still exist? One thing was for sure, it was going to be a very long day of classes.

4.

That afternoon at lunch, as Nellie and the boys sat at their normal table eating their bagged lunches, they couldn't stop talking about the big news.

"This is so awesome!" said Johnny, scarfing down his peanut-butter-and-Nutella sandwich. "Just think, somewhere right here in our town is the remains of a real Delaware chief—a murdered one! I haven't been this excited since Witch Flavor added gummy worms to their ice cream condiment selection."

"Yeah, boy," replied Bubba sarcastically. "That sure was huge. I can't believe it wasn't trending on Twitter." He and Logan shared a big laugh as Johnny responded by sticking out his peanut-butter-and-Nutella-covered tongue.

Nellie was in no mood for kidding around. "Johnny is right," she said. "Disgusting, but right. This really is a big deal. And there's something else I haven't told you: I think *History Hunters* is actually here for the amulet!" She then told the boys about what she had heard while eavesdropping on Rick Jenson the previous day.

Logan was the first to respond. "Of all the duplicitous, reprehensible, diabolical—"

"I believe 'jerk' is the word you're looking for," Bubba interjected.

"Wow," said Johnny. "But he seems so nice on the show."

"Well, he's not," said Nellie. "And if I'm right, he couldn't care less about honoring Pisquetomen. He's just after the amulet, which I assume has gotta be worth a ton of money."

"And what if it really is magical, like they say?" added Logan.

"Oh, please," said Bubba. "A magical stone? I tell you what, if you believe that, I got a whole box of magic stones I found down by the river last week. I'll sell 'em to you—*real* cheap. Magic amulet—ha!"

"Magic or not," replied Nellie, "why should we let them find it? After all, Pis-keh...Pis-keh..."

"Tomen," offered Logan.

"Right. Thanks. Pisquetomen lived here. In our town! It's a part of our history, and I for one think we should be able to keep it."

"Who says they're planning on keeping it?" said Bubba.

"Who says they aren't?" replied Nellie.

Johnny agreed. "Right! I know if I found a magical stone, I wouldn't be donating it to any old museum. A thing like that would have to be pretty valuable...like the Pope Diamond!"

Bubba's head dropped to his hands. "It's the Hope Diamond, you moron. *Hope*, not *Pope!*"

Johnny frowned. "Hope? That doesn't make any sense. You sure?"

"Yes," said Nellie. "He's sure. Now let's focus on what's important! How are we going to find that stone before they do?"

When the final bell rang, Nellie and the boys grabbed their backpacks and ran all the way to Bubba's house along Water Street, catty-corner from the Fort Brodhead site. As they sat around the kitchen counter sipping cans of orange Fanta, none of them had any idea what they were going to do next. One thing was for sure: they had to come up with a plan to find the grave of Pisquetomen before Rick Jenson and the *History Hunters* did.

"OK," said Logan, "the first thing we need to do is find a detailed site plan of the fort. I'm sure the historical society has one in its archives. Then we'll draw a grid on the plan, which will enable us to do an orderly and systematic search for the grave site."

Nellie rolled her eyes.

"And how exactly do we search for this grave, Logan?" asked Bubba. "Should we go out and rent an old-Indian-grave detector or something?"

Johnny laughed, causing orange pop to come out of his nose.

"Ew," said Nellie. "Gross."

Bubba continued. "And then what? Even if by some miracle we're able to locate the grave, we can't just go digging up a historic site. Besides, aren't graves, like, six feet down or somethin'? That sounds like a lot of work, if you ask me."

"Actually," said Logan, "yes, modern graves

are usually six feet deep, as a rule. But that's because they have to make it deep enough for the casket and the cement sarcophagus. In this case, however—"

"Ugh! Who cares?" interrupted Nellie. "We don't have time to analyze site plans or do grid searches or whatever else you had in mind. Those guys probably already know where it is—and we gotta figure out a way to stop them!"

"And how to you propose we do that, Miss Smarty-pants?" said Johnny.

But before Nellie could reply, there was a knock at the front door. Bubba opened it to see a man in a uniform from the gas company.

"Well, hello there, young man," he said. "Is your mommy or daddy home?"

"No," replied Bubba. "They're not home from work yet. Pretty soon, though."

"Oh. Well, I'm from the gas company, and we need to do an inspection of your interior line to make sure there's no leaks or anything. Mind if I come in?"

Bubba hesitated for a moment. After all, his mom did tell him not to open the door for strangers, let alone let them inside the house. But this guy looked legit, and Bubba's friends were all here, too. "Sure," Bubba replied. "C'mon, I'll show you where the basement is."

As Bubba let the man inside and led him through the foyer toward the basement door, Nellie turned to look and immediately did a double take. "Did you see that guy?" she whispered to Logan and Johnny, who were still discussing modern burial techniques.

"Yeah. What about him?" asked Johnny. "Looks like Keanu Reeves, if you ask me."

"You're right!" replied Logan. "He does! By the way, why are we whispering?"

Nellie made sure Bubba and the man had gone downstairs before she answered. "There's... just something about him. I swear I know him from somewhere."

"OK," said Johnny, "so you know the gas man. So what?"

Nellie crept over to the top of the basement stairs to see if she could hear anything.

"What's your deal?" said Bubba, emerging from behind the basement door.

"Come here!" whispered Nellie, dragging him back into the kitchen. "That guy down there...

are you sure he's with the gas company? I know I've seen him somewhere before."

Bubba looked confused. "That guy? Yeah, he's legit. Kinda looks like Keanu Reeves though."

"That's what I was just saying!" said Johnny. "Weird, right?"

"I don't know," said Nellie, "something's just not right about that guy."

Meanwhile, Logan got back to brainstorming. "All right," he said, "I can see your point about locating the grave. The fort site is huge—approximately 350 feet wide by 200 feet deep. It would take forever to search it systematically. What we need is to find some written record of the burial and then see if we can pinpoint the general area where they may have buried old Mr. P."

"Mr. P?" said Bubba. "So that's what we're calling him now?"

"Yes," Logan replied. "That way no one will know who we're talking about."

"Good idea!" said Johnny. "But shouldn't we at least call him Chief P? You know, out of respect?"

Bubba and Logan both rolled their eyes.

As the boys continued the discussion, Nellie tiptoed her way back over to the door to the basement and slowly opened it. Quietly, she made her way down the stairs to see if she could get a better look at the man. As she reached the bottom step, she heard a voice and turned to see the man over in the corner by one of the basement walls talking on his cell phone.

"Yeah," he said in a hushed voice, "I'm in the basement right now. I think I know where to look, but it's not gonna be easy. These old stone walls have all been plastered over."

Nellie tried to creep a little closer so she could hear the man better. But as she tiptoed past some old paint cans, she accidentally kicked one that was half empty, making a loud noise.

Immediately the man spun around and spotted Nellie not twenty feet away. "Look, I gotta go," he said into his phone before slipping it into his pocket.

Nellie locked eyes with the man. His gaze sent a chill up her spine. She turned and darted back up the steps and into the kitchen.

"There you are," said Logan. "We thought you went home or something."

Nellie looked back over her shoulder just to be sure she wasn't being followed. "I don't know who that guy really is, but he was talking on his phone to someone about looking for something down there!"

"Uh, yeah," said Bubba. "He's looking for the gas line. That's what the gas company does. What's with you today?"

Just then the man shut the basement door and walked over to the foyer. "Well," he said to Bubba. "I didn't find any leaks. So that's good. Other than that, just let your folks know we'll probably be back tomorrow to install a new line, just as a precaution."

"Will do," said Bubba, opening the door to let the man out. But before leaving, the man turned and took one last good look at Nellie.

"Have a nice day," he said, walking out the door and toward a white van parked in front. Nellie jumped up and ran to the front window just in time to see the vehicle pull away and disappear down the street.

"See, Nellie," said Bubba. "Like I said, nice guy."

"I'm telling you," Nellie replied, "there's something not right about that guy. He was looking for something down there—and it wasn't any gas leak! I just know it."

"Well, I'm telling *you* that there's nothing down there but the furnace, some spiders, and a bunch of my folks' old junk."

Nellie, however, wasn't so sure. But now that the man was gone, she sat back down with the boys to map out their plan.

5.

Later that afternoon the four of them were down at the McIntosh Memorial Library looking for clues. Located along Water Street, just down the road from the fort site, the library was a treasure-trove of information. In addition to offering online access to all the town's old newspapers, it also had an entire section in the back corner dedicated to local history. This was one of Nellie's favorite places to hang out. Many an afternoon she sat on the floor near the stacks, perusing the old books, looking at the old photographs, and discovering interesting stories about the town and its people. It was like having her very own personal time machine.

Today, however, Nellie had more pressing

things on her mind. As she and Bubba pored through books on the area, looking for anything about Pisquetomen, Johnny and Logan sat at a nearby table looking over an old the map of the fort, searching for anything that might signify a burial.

"Aw, it's no use," said Johnny, frustrated. "This is the same old map we've seen a hundred times before. And I never saw any graveyard or anything on it."

Nellie looked up from her book. "They wouldn't have buried him in an actual graveyard, silly. They were trying to hide the burial site, remember?"

"Oh yeah, that's right!"

"Shhh!" The librarian glared at them from her desk, pressing her finger to her lips. Johnny mouthed the word "sorry" and continued to scan the map.

Bubba was growing frustrated too as he flipped through one of the first histories of the fort. "I'm not seeing anything in here," he said. "I don't know. Maybe the whole thing's just a made-up story."

"Just keep looking," said Nellie, as she carefully scanned the names in a copy of the fort's original log book. "There's gotta be something, anything—some clue that will give us a general idea of where Mr. P might be buried."

A couple of hours went by. Mentally exhausted, the kids were about to call it a day when Nellie's eyes suddenly lit up. "Here it is!" she said. "I found it!"

The librarian shushed them again. Nellie flashed an apologetic smile and then turned back to the book, a copy of a journal of one of the fort's officers. "Look!" she said. "Right here... June 20, 1780... 'We buried O.W.E. in the yard today near the northeast bastion. It was a swift, quiet affair overseen by Major Wilson.'"

"So that's it?" asked Logan. "Nothing else?"

"But we don't need anything else!" said Nellie. "Don't you see? O.W.E. That has to be Old White Eye!" She moved over to the table where the map was still open. "Look...here's the northeast bastion. The 'yard' must be the area just outside the fence."

Johnny moved in for a closer look. "Yeah. Sounds about right. But it just says *near* the bastion. That's still a big area to search."

"True," said Logan. "But the possible search area is a heck of a lot smaller than it was before. All we have to do now is locate this general area here, and then we can enact our original grid search plan."

Bubba huffed. "Lotta good that'll do us. Think about it: we can't just go digging around in a national historic site!"

"Yeah," replied Johnny. "I'm sure *History Hunters* has special permission or somethin'. But if someone sees a bunch of kids with shovels..."

"Wait a second," Bubba interrupted. "Where'd you say this 'yard' is supposed to be again?"

Nellie placed a finger on the map showing the location of the northeast bastion. "Somewhere near here. Why?"

"Well," said Bubba, "we're gonna have a heck of a time finding anything buried there."

The other three leaned in for a closer look. "I don't get it," said Logan. "Seems pretty feasible to me. The bastion location is clearly marked here. All we need to do is pinpoint it using the GPS app on my phone."

"Oh, really?" said Bubba. "Then tell me this, Einstein. How are we gonna dig under someone's house? The northeast bastion would be on the *other* side of Water Street—right where there are three houses now, including mine."

"Oh, that's right," said Logan. "I guess I didn't consider that."

"Heck," continued Bubba, "chances are they dug up old Mr. P's bones long ago back in the late 1800s when those houses were built."

Just then an older girl they recognized from their school walked over to their table.

"Hey," she said, "did you guys hear?"

"Hear what?" replied Nellie.

"*History Hunters* is filming over at Bug Park. They've got a whole setup—cameras, lights, a big tent. It's really cool!"

Johnny looked confused. "Bug Park? I don't get it. Why would they be way over there and not at the fort site?"

"Beats me," said the girl. "But I guess they're looking for extras, so we're heading over. You guys comin'?"

"Thanks," replied Nellie. "Maybe we'll see you guys there." As the girl walked away, Nellie turned back to the map. "I think you're right about the houses, Bubba. The road would be right here today, cutting the fort site pretty much in half. I can't believe they'd let anyone build a house there, though."

"Remember, Nellie," said Logan, "it wasn't until the mid-1900s that anyone showed any interest in preserving the fort site. I guess they thought it was as boring as you do."

"OK," she replied, "I'm sorry about the 'boring' comment. I admit it. I was wrong. But I still can't believe we might have lost such a historical treasure just to make room for someone's basement. No offense, Bubba. Bubba?" Nellie suddenly noticed that it was just she and Logan hovering over the map. "Hey, where'd they go?"

Logan's phone pinged. "Bug Park is my guess," he said, holding up the text message from Johnny saying he and Bubba were already on their way there.

"All right," said Nellie. "Let's go. We've learned all we can here, I guess."

And with that she and Logan headed out to catch up with their friends.

6.

Nellie and the boys skidded their bikes to a stop as they arrived at Bug Park. Its actual name was Washington Square, but the playground equipment resembled giant insects, so everyone had always just called it Bug Park. Today it might have well been called Hollywood Park, with all the lights and cameras, not to mention all the production people buzzing around.

"Whoa!" said Johnny. "This is so cool. I can't believe they're actually filming a show in our favorite park!"

Nellie thought it was pretty awesome, too. But she had other things on her mind. "I don't get it. Why are they here? Nothing historic ever happened here at the park, as far as I know."

"Sure it did," Bubba chimed in.

"Really?" said Logan.

"Yeah, don't you remember? This is where Johnny made history by crapping his pants during a pick-up football game. It's legendary."

Johnny frowned. "Ha-ha. Very funny, Bubba. And by the way, I didn't *crap* my pants. Just had a little accident, is all."

"Look!" said Logan. "Over by the tent—there's Rick Jenson! Wow. The host of *History Hunters*, right here in our park. A momentous day, indeed!"

As the kids all looked on, Mr. Vincent walked up to greet them. "Well, if it isn't my favorite little history buffs! Come to see if maybe you could get on TV, huh?"

Nellie turned and smiled politely. "Hey, Mr. Vincent."

"Hey, Mr. Vincent!" echoed the boys in unison.

"We were just checking it out," said Nellie. "Thing is, we can't figure out why they'd be filming here in Bug Park."

"Why not?" said Mr. Vincent. "After all, this is one of the most historic sites in town."

The kids all looked confused.

"It is?" said Bubba.

"Sure. I'd say the site of the town's first burial ground is pretty significant, wouldn't you?"

Now Nellie was even more confused. "But, Mr. Vincent, I thought the first cemetery was way over on the other end of town, near the school."

"Yeah," said Johnny. "At least that's what they told us back in third grade when we went there on a field trip."

Mr. Vincent took a seat on a park bench. "Yes, Johnny, that was the town's first *official* cemetery," he said. "But this is where the first burials actually took place. You remember in class when we talked about how they hanged those poor soldiers for trying to desert the fort?"

The kids all nodded together.

"Well," said Mr. Vincent, "supposedly, this is where they buried them. At least that's the best we can figure based on the commander's journal."

"No way!" said Johnny. "A burial ground—here! Just think, we've been playing on top of dead bodies all this time!"

"And crapping on them, too," added Bubba, much to Johnny's chagrin.

"OK," said Nellie, "but that still doesn't explain why they'd be filming here. I mean, they're supposed to be looking for Pisquetomen, not some deserters' graves."

Right then Nellie saw a familiar man walk out of the big tent and start heading across the park. "Look!" she said. "It's him!"

The boys and Mr. Vincent all turned to look in the direction Nellie was pointing.

"Him who?" said Bubba.

"The man! That guy who came to your house and was snooping around in your basement, remember? Keanu Reeves! I knew he wasn't with the gas company!"

"Oh yeah!" replied Bubba. "You're right. That's weird. Wonder what he's doing here?"

Mr. Vincent seemed confused. "Wait..who's Keanu Reeves? And why was he in Bubba's house? Isn't that man just one of the *History Hunters* crew?"

Logan looked shocked. "Are you kidding me, Mr. Vincent? Who's Keanu Reeves? Um...'The Matrix.' 'John Wick'—"

"'Edward Scissorhands,'" added Johnny.

Bubba sighed. "That wasn't Keanu Reeves, you dope. That was Johnny Depp!"

"Oh, yeah! My bad."

Mr. Vincent shrugged. "Sorry, Bubba. I guess I'm just not much of a movie guy. Unless, that is, we're talking about 'Casablanca.' Now that's a movie."

Nellie, however, was still focused on the Gas Man. "Listen, Mr. V. That man was at Bubba's house earlier today wearing a Columbia Gas uniform and..." Nellie paused as she watched the man get into a white van and start heading down the alley next to the park. "Oh, no—he's leaving!"

"Yeah," said Logan. "So what?"

"So we have to follow him and see where he's going!" Nellie jumped back on her bike. "C'mon!"

But just as the boys went to pick up their bikes, one of the show's crew came over to them.

"Hey, kids!" she said. "We're looking for a few extras for today's shoot. How would you guys like to be on TV?"

Nellie was tempted, but she really wanted to find out who that man was. "Uh, thanks," she began, "but we—"

"We'll get to be on TV?" asked Johnny.

The woman nodded.

"Sweet! Count me in!"

"Me too!" said Logan.

"Do we get free food?" asked Bubba.

"Sure! You're more than welcome to grab a sandwich in the tent, after we get done with the shoot, of course."

Nellie couldn't believe what she was hearing. "You guys! What are you doing? We can't stay here. We gotta follow that van!"

But the boys had already set their bikes back down and were following the crew member over to the filming area.

"Eh," said Bubba over his shoulder, "we'll never be able to catch up with him now anyways."

Nellie turned back toward the van just in time to see it disappear around the corner. *Great,* she thought. *There goes our chance.* She turned back around to finish telling Mr. Vincent about the gas man incident, but now he too was walking toward the tent. "Mr. Vincent! Where are you going?"

Her teacher stopped and turned around. "Oh, I just thought I'd see if they could use an old fuddy-duddy like me as an extra. Either way," he added with a wink, "I'll get a free sandwich out of it. You comin'?"

Nellie really wanted to figure out where the

mysterious man was headed, but the white van was already long gone. Having the chance to be on her favorite TV show wasn't a bad alternative. "Sure," she replied. "Why not?" She set her bike down on the grass and joined Mr. Vincent.

In her mind, though, she couldn't help but wonder where that white van was headed.

7.

"Man, that was so cool!" said Johnny.

It was almost dinnertime now, and after a long afternoon of filming at the park, he and the other kids were pedaling their bikes back to Bubba's house.

Logan beamed as his BMX glided along the smooth asphalt surface of Water Street. "I know! Just think—we're actually going to be on an episode of *History Hunters!*"

"It was all right, I guess," said Bubba, chomping on another Popsicle stick as he steered his mountain bike down the street. "I'm just glad we got some free grub out of the deal."

"Yeah," added Johnny. "And who knows? Maybe we'll get nominated for a Grammy or somethin'!"

Bubba and Logan looked at each other and shook their heads.

"What?" asked Johnny. "It's a perfectly reasonable question."

While the boys were chatting, Nellie kept pretty much to herself. She was excited too, but she couldn't help but think about the Gas Man. Where was he going when she last saw him leaving Bug Park? She had no idea what he was up to, but she was certain it was no good. And she knew they had to figure it out as soon as possible.

As the four of them approached Bubba's house, Johnny yelled out, "Hey! Check it out!"

The others looked up and saw that the street in front of Bubba's house was completely blocked off by orange construction cones and yellow caution tape. A police cruiser was also parked in the middle of the road with its flashing lights on.

Bubba rode up to his mother, who was standing out on the neighbor's sidewalk talking on her phone. "Hey, Mom, what gives? How come our house is all taped up?"

"Yes, thank you, I'll hold," Mrs. Thompson spoke into her phone before turning to Bubba.

"Everything's OK, honey. The gas company just detected some sort of leak around our house, and they want to make sure it's safe."

Bubba turned to look at his house, which now looked like a crime scene with all the yellow tape around it. "A gas leak—geez. When are they gonna let us back in?"

"I'm sorry, honey, but I don't think we'll be able to go back in until tomorrow at the earliest. I'm on the line with the Holiday Inn right now trying to reserve a room for tonight."

"A hotel? But Mom, I—"

"Oh, hello, yes—I'm still here." Mrs. Thompson waved her son off as she walked further down the sidewalk.

The sound of a car door closing caught Nellie's attention. She turned to see a man emerge from a van—a white van!—parked right across the street from Bubba's house. The man, who was carrying some type of metal case, quickly made his way up the front walk and went inside.

"It's him!" cried Nellie. "Keanu Reeves! I knew it! I just knew he was up to something."

"Are you sure?" asked Logan.

"I'm positive! It's the same guy I saw at the

press conference, in Bubba's basement, and then over again at Bug Park!"

"Maybe he works for the film crew *and* the gas company," Johnny offered. "My uncle Freddy used to work for the water authority during the day and as a janitor for the Episcopal church at night."

Bubba groaned. "You idiot! How could he work for the gas company here in McIntosh and at the same time be flying all over the country with the *History Hunters* crew?"

Johnny shrugged. "It was just a theory."

Nellie, however, didn't need any other theories. "There's definitely something fishy going on here. And we're going to find out just what." She set her bike down on the grass and turned to Johnny and Logan. "You two stay here and keep Mrs. Thompson busy. C'mon, Bubba!" She started running around the back of the neighbor's house.

"What?" said Bubba, stepping off his bike and laying it on the ground. "Wait up! Where are we going?"

"Just c'mon!"

While Mrs. Thompson was distracted on her

phone, Bubba and Nellie snuck along the narrow path that led between the back of the neighbor's house and a line of tall shrubs. As they reached the end of the house, they crouched down in the shade and looked over at Bubba's backyard, which, just like the front, was completely lined with caution tape.

"OK," said Bubba, "now what?"

"Remember that time you had that sleepover on your birthday and we snuck out through the basement window to run up the street for a pop at Scotty's News?"

"Yeah, so?"

"So, is the basement window still unlocked?"

"I think so, why?"

"Good. 'Cause that's how were gonna sneak in there and figure out just what Mr. Gas Man is up to."

Bubba peered over at his house. "I don't know, Nellie. Isn't it against the law to cross caution tape?"

"Yeah, but only if it's a *real* emergency. There's no leak at your house, Bubba. I'm positive. And that guy definitely doesn't work for the gas company. I think he's here looking for the amulet!"

Bubba wasn't convinced. "I don't know..."

Nellie knew exactly what to say next. "Since when are you the one to follow rules? You're starting to sound like Logan. What's wrong? Scared?"

That made Bubba perk up. "Scared? Of what? To go into my own house? Yeah, right. Follow me."

8.

Bubba and Nellie darted across the yard and under the caution tape to the basement window. Taking one last look around, just to make sure they weren't being watched, the two of them crouched down and peered in through the dirty window.

"Dang it, I can't see anything," whispered Nellie, cupping her hands on the window glass. "We're going to have to get inside."

Bubba let out a sigh. "OK," he said. "Just remember, we gotta be real quiet. I'll go in first and help you down."

The lock on the basement window had been broken as long as Bubba could remember. All he had to do was give the old metal frame a little tug and it squeaked open.

Nellie's eyes grew wide. "Shhhh!"

"I know, I know," Bubba mouthed. Then, very carefully, he climbed in through the opening and lowered himself down to the cement floor. The lights were on and he could hear some strange noises coming from the other end of the basement, but there was no sign of the man or anyone else. Turning back to the window, Bubba waved Nellie in and helped her down.

As soon as she hit the floor, Nellie scanned her surroundings. "See anyone?" she whispered.

Bubba pointed to the back corner of the basement on the other side of the stairs. "I think someone's over there. Listen..."

The two of them could hear a scraping type of sound accompanied by an occasional grunt. Then came the loud grinding noise of some type of power tool. Now was their chance to get a little closer while the sound covered their movement.

Keeping as low as possible, they scooted along the wall past the water softener and a dusty old pile of paint cans. Nellie brushed a cobweb away from her face as she slowly peered around the corner. There he was—the Gas Man! His back was to them as he operated a drill, pushing it into the basement wall and sending bits of rock flying and falling to the floor. Setting the drill on the ground, the man picked up a small brush and started using it on the wall where he'd been drilling. As the dust began to settle, Nellie couldn't believe her eyes. There in the wall, plain as day, were some bones and what appeared to be a skull—a human skull!

Nellie spun around to tell Bubba, but the sound of footsteps on the stairs had caused him to panic and take off for the window. In doing so he tripped on the paint cans, which made a loud noise and sent him crashing to the floor.

"Hey! What's going on down there?" came a voice from the stairway.

Nellie turned to follow her friend, but just as she did a hand grabbed her shirt from behind. Spinning around, she looked up into the dusty, unshaven face of the Gas Man.

Another man turned the corner from the stairs. "Hey!" he said. "What are you kids doing in here? Don't you know there's a leak?"

Bubba picked himself up from the cement floor and tried to come up with something. "Uh, yeah, well...this is my house, and we were just, uh..."

"You're lying!" Nellie broke in. "There's no leak!" She turned and scowled at her captor. "And you! You aren't from the gas company, either. I know who you *really* are and what you're doing here. You're looking for the amulet!"

Nellie's accusation seemed to rattle the other man. "What?" he stammered. "Amulet? That's crazy. What would make you kids think that—"

But the Gas Man was in no mood for games. "Get 'em outta here!" he growled, shoving Nellie toward the other man.

"You won't get away with this!" said Nellie. "That amulet belongs to us! To our town! It's our history!"

But before she could say anything else, the other man grabbed her and Bubba by their arms. "C'mon, you two," he said, pulling them up the stairs and then out the front door.

Bubba's mom had just gotten off the phone and was talking with the other boys when the man brought Bubba and Nellie over.

"Found these two snooping around in the basement," he said. "Better keep them away from that house. It's not safe." Then he turned and walked back toward the house.

"Robert Milton Thompson!" said Bubba's

mom. "What in the world were you thinking? You could've been asphyxiated!"

Bubba put his head down in shame.

"And Nellie...I mean, I know my son doesn't always make the best decisions, but I certainly expected more of you."

"But Mrs. Thompson," replied Nellie, "those men...they're not from the gas company! They're trying to steal Pisquetomen's amulet!"

Bubba's mom looked confused. "Pis-keh-who's what?" she replied. "No, dear, I think you're mistaken. It's just a little gas leak is all. Now, you and your friends need to go home and let these men do their job."

"She's telling the truth, Mrs. Thompson!" said Logan.

"*Milton?*" said Johnny, laughing. "Your middle name is *Milton?* You gotta be kidding me, Bubba...I mean, excuse me, Robert!"

Bubba wasn't amused. "You better just shut it, Johnny. Nobody calls me Robert except for my mother. Nobody!"

"Johnny! Bubba! Enough!"

"Sorry, Nellie," replied Bubba.

"She's right, Mrs. Thompson," said Johnny.

"You just gotta believe us!"

But Bubba's mom wasn't hearing any of it. "That'll be enough, Johnny. That's enough from all of you. You kids run along now. These men have work to do." Then, grabbing Bubba by the arm, she said, "And you, young man...you're coming with me! We're going to the hotel."

"But Mom!" Bubba said, turning to his friends as his mother pulled him down the sidewalk toward their car.

Meanwhile, Nellie turned to look at Bubba's house just as the Gas Man came out the front door carrying a metal case.

"Look!" said Johnny "What do you think he's got in there?"

Nellie let out a sigh. "I'll give you three guesses."

Logan turned to look at her. "You mean... the amulet?"

But Nellie didn't respond. She was too busy thinking about what to do next. "C'mon, you guys!" she said, running over to her bike.

"Why?" said Logan. "Where are we going now?

"We gotta find Mr. Vincent," replied Nellie. "He's the only one who'll believe us. He'll know what to do!"

9.

Mr. Vincent lived in a modest, wood-framed house on the quiet, still-wooded side of town. According to him, it was one of the oldest homes in McIntosh, built with beams from the old fort itself. Over time, as settlers moved into the area, this little corner of town managed to remain somewhat secluded. A quiet little stream called Two Mile Run flowed through the backyard and ran all the way to the river. Behind the house was nothing but hills and woods all the way up to Gypsy Glen Road.

Nellie and the boys arrived at the house out of breath. They dropped their bikes on Mr. Vincent's front lawn and ran around back, where they found their teacher sitting on the back porch smoking his pipe.

"Mr. Vincent! Mr. Vincent!" said Nellie, huffing and puffing.

"Whoa! Whoa!" he said, taking the pipe from his mouth. "What happened? The dam break?"

"It's the amulet," Logan broke in. "They have it!"

"The amulet? Who's this *they* you're talking about?"

"The *History Hunters* people," said Nellie. "They were digging under Bubba's house, inside the basement, and they found Pisquetomen's grave! We saw them leaving the house with a metal suitcase, and we think they might have found the amulet!"

"Oh," chuckled Mr. Vincent, "I highly doubt that."

Nellie was confused. "But I was down in the basement with Bubba. We saw the grave and there was this skull and everything and—"

Mr. Vincent put his hand up to stop her as he puffed on his pipe. "Like I said, I highly doubt they found the amulet."

"How can you be so sure?" asked Logan.

"Well, because it was found years ago, and I know who has it."

Nellie's mouth fell open. "Wait...what? You know who has the amulet? Who?"

"Why, Roger Appletree, of course," replied Mr. Vincent.

"Roger who?" all three children responded in unison.

"Appletree. You know, the co-director of the McIntosh Area Historical Society.

Johnny looked confused. "Wait...you mean the old guy that carries around that...that wizard staff thingy with him everywhere he goes? That guy?"

"Well, yes," Mr. Vincent replied, "he does use a hand-carved cane ever since he was wounded in the war, but I wouldn't necessarily call him *old*. He's right around my age. Unless, that is, you consider me old." He gave Johnny a wink before taking another puff on his pipe.

Nellie took a seat on the bench next to him. "But, Mr. Vincent, I don't understand. How did Roger...I mean, Mr. Appletree get the amulet? And why would the *History Hunters* people come here looking for it if it's already been found?"

"Well, because no one knew about it besides Roger and yours truly. And now you three, of course. It all began back in the early 1970s, during the excavation of the old fort site..."

Over the next few minutes, Mr. Vincent told

Nellie and the boys how back during the archaeological dig, they hired Mr. Applegate for his expertise in Native American artifacts. An actual descendant of the Turkey Clan of the Delaware—Pisquetomen's tribe—he wanted to make sure if any artifacts were found that they were properly catalogued and preserved. During the dig, Mr. Appletree personally discovered the grave of Pisquetomen, which he recognized due to the green amulet he found along with the remains. Not wanting the amulet to fall into the wrong hands, he secreted it away until he could figure out what exactly should be done with it.

"But, I don't get it," said Logan. "Why didn't he want anyone to know about it?"

"Yeah," said Johnny, "why not just put it in the museum with all the other stuff they found at the site?"

Mr. Vincent sat back in his chair. "You kids have to understand, being a Delaware himself, Roger felt a special connection to the amulet. Among his people it's a sacred object that belonged to one of their most respected ancestors. He didn't feel right having it put on display in some dusty old museum. It simply means too much to him and his people." All three kids sat quietly, letting Mr. Vincent's words sink in. "Plus, if he'd have left it in the grave with the rest of Pisquetomen, they might have ended up exhuming the old chief's remains and putting both him and the amulet on display. And Roger just couldn't let that happen. By taking the amulet, he protected Pisquetomen's anonymity, and therefore, his remains were left undisturbed just like any others they found at the site."

"You mean, there were others buried there, too?"

"Yes, Johnny," replied Mr. Vincent. "Quite a few, actually. Life was hard on the edge of the frontier. There were accidents. Soldiers got sick. I'm afraid death was quite common at the old fort."

Nellie smiled. "So whoever's skeleton they found in Bubba's basement...it couldn't have been Mr. P!"

"Mr. P?" asked Mr. Vincent.

"That's just what we call Pisquetomen for short," replied Johnny.

Mr. Vincent smiled. "Oh, I see. And you're correct, Nellie. Whoever's grave they found in Bubba's basement certainly wasn't that of Pisquetomen. His was uncovered on the other side of the street where the fort memorial is today."

"So nobody knows about the amulet but you and Mr. Appletree?" asked Nellie.

"Correct," said Mr. Vincent. "And now that you three know as well, I trust that it will remain our little secret, yes?"

"Don't worry, Mr. V. You can trust us." But even as Nellie was saying this, she knew exactly where they'd be heading next—the McIntosh Area Historical Society.

10.

By the time Nellie and the boys had left Mr. Vincent's, the historical society was closed for the night. But first thing after school the next day, all four of them hopped on their bikes and headed straight there.

Housed in the former P&LE train station across town, the McIntosh Area Historical Society was an award-winning museum that worked to preserve and celebrate the town's rich heritage. In addition to housing hundreds of historical items from the town, it was also a popular destination for school field trips and out-of-towners looking to learn more about the area.

It only took the kids a few minutes to get to the historical society from their school, as they took the shortcut through the old cemetery and down Gypsy Glen Road. But just as they turned the last corner by Don's Deli, Nellie slammed on her brakes, nearly causing a multi-bicycle pile-up.

"Geez, Nellie!" said Bubba, who just barely swerved out of the way in time. "How about a little warning next time?"

"Look!" Nellie replied, pointing across the street at the historical society. "It's them! They beat us here!"

Bubba and the boys turned to see a line of three *History Hunters* SUVs parked along the street outside the museum.

"I don't get it," said Johnny. "What are they doing here? I thought Mr. Vincent said no one else knew Mr. Appletree had the stone."

Just then the front door of the museum opened and Rick Jenson stepped out.

"Get back!" Nellie said, dragging her bike around the side of the deli building.

"What are we hiding from?" asked Logan.

"Yeah, it's just your boyfriend Rick and his crew."

Nellie wasn't amused. "We can't afford them seeing us here. If the Gas Man has talked to

Rick—and I'm sure he has by now—he already knows we know too much!"

"So what if he does?" Bubba replied. "They're a TV show crew, for cryin' out loud. What are they gonna do, film us to death?"

"Laugh it up, you guys," said Nellie. "But I don't trust that Rick Jenson. And I definitely don't trust you-know-who. Magical or not, that amulet has to be worth some big bucks. And when there's money involved, you're sure to attract some shady characters."

Nellie peeked around the corner of the building as the last of the *History Hunters* vans pulled away from the museum. "C'mon!" she said. "Let's go talk to Mr. Appletree. Hopefully he didn't tell them about the amulet."

Roger Appletree's office sat in a cozy little corner of the museum's main floor. Piles of paper covered his desk, behind which he spent most days doing research and writing for the society's quarterly newsletter. All around him were bookshelves packed to the ceiling with volumes on local history and old photographs of days gone by.

The kids all reached the museum's front door

at the same time and came tumbling in. Roger stood up from his desk, grabbed his cane, and walked over to greet them.

"Well, good afternoon!" he said. "You got here just in time. Usually we close up right about now, but I guess we can make an exception today."

"Good afternoon, Mr. Appletree. My name's Logan. We met you last year when our class came here on a tour. And these are my friends Bubba, Johnny, and Nellie."

Roger smiled and shook Logan's hand. "Ah, yes! I thought you all looked familiar. What brings you kids in today?"

"Well, we were just—"

"What can you tell us about Pisquetomen?" Nellie cut off Logan and got right down to business.

Mr. Appletree was visibly surprised. "Well," he began, "it seems the old Delaware chief is quite popular today. You're the second group of folks to come in here asking about him."

"You mean the *History Hunters?*" asked Nellie. "Is that why they were here? Please don't tell me you gave them the amulet!"

"The amulet? How do you kids know about

the amulet?"

Logan scrambled for a reply. "Well...uh... we're just big local history buffs, I guess."

"Apparently so," replied Roger. "Not many people around here know about it. That said, I didn't give those people the amulet or anything else, for that matter."

Nellie and the boys all smiled and sighed with relief.

"After all, how could I give them something I don't even have?"

"But Mr. Vin—" Johnny caught himself. "Um...I mean...we heard that the amulet might be here...with you."

"Oh, it was at one time," Roger replied. "Just not anymore."

"Well, if you don't have it," asked Bubba, "then where is it?"

Roger turned around and began back toward his office. "Look, kids, I'm very busy. If you have a question about our current display or maybe about the old fort, I'd be glad to help, but—"

"Please, Mr. Appletree!" Nellie walked over next to him. "Those men from *History Hunters* are trying to find the amulet. And if they do, I'm afraid they'll take it away from here, from the town of McIntosh—where it belongs! We just want to be sure it's safe."

Roger paused for a moment, and then, turning to Logan, he said, "Do me a favor, son. Go and lock the door. Then maybe we can have a little chat about the amulet."

11.

"So we were right!" said Nellie, admiring the hundreds of titles that lined the built-in bookshelves in Roger's office. "That's why the *History Hunters* crew was here—they were looking for the amulet!"

"Yes," replied Roger. "But not in so many words. They asked me about Pisquetomen, of course, and if I had an opinion on where I thought he might be buried."

"What did you tell them?" asked Logan.

"Oh, you know, just the old stories. About how some say he died at the fort and others say he migrated west into Ohio."

"But you know what really happened to him, don't you?"

"Yes, Nellie. I do."

"What about the amulet?" asked Bubba. "You really don't have it?"

"No, Bubba. I don't. But even if I did, I wouldn't tell you. No offense."

Nellie was visibly frustrated. "It doesn't make sense," she said. "It's a local treasure, a part of our heritage—a part of *your* heritage. Why not display it for local people to admire and be proud of? Something as important as the amulet would draw a ton of visitors to your museum. Don't you think?"

"Yeah," Logan agreed. "And from the looks of this place, you could use a few more visitors. No offense."

Roger allowed a little grin to grow on his face. "You're right about that, Logan. This place could definitely use a new coat of paint and whatnot. And, yes, Nellie, the amulet would certainly be a big draw. But some things are more important, more sacred, than money. That's why I hid it somewhere safe, where it will never be disturbed again. That stone isn't to be messed with. Besides, I didn't want to see it fall into the wrong hands."

"What do you mean by that?" asked Bubba. "You don't really believe the stone has magical powers, do you? I mean, that's just fairy-tale stuff."

Roger's face grew serious. "I wouldn't be so sure, young man. Chief Pisquetomen was a mysterious man with even more mysterious abilities. There are tales of him disappearing—seemingly into thin air—and then reappearing somewhere far away, as if he had mastered the power of teleportation."

"Whoa!"

"Whoa is right, Johnny. Furthermore, as a guide for the British emissary, Pisquetomen somehow always managed to escape unharmed from even the most precarious of situations. It was almost as if he could read and control other people's minds. And apparently he healed incredibly quickly too—unnaturally so. Legend has it that the chief was shot on at least two occasions but somehow recovered within days and was none the worse for it."

"And you believe that the amulet gave him these powers?" asked Logan.

"Well, I can't be certain. But for the brief time that I was in possession of the stone...well, all I can say is that I could definitely sense some type of strange energy, and I had an uneasy feeling about it."

"But what if those guys come back here and force you to tell them where it is?" asked Nellie. "Believe me, they'll try just about anything to get that stone."

Roger laughed. "I'm not worried about that."

"Well, you should be," said Bubba. "They broke into my house and pretended to be the gas company just so they could look for it. Nellie's right. These guys are bad news."

Still, Roger seemed unfazed. "Oh, I believe you about that. I could tell there was something off about them. But I'm not concerned. After all, the amulet's not anywhere near the museum." That got the kids' attention. "I buried it safely inside an old forgotten Delaware cave many, many years ago. And there it will stay."

"Cave?" said Johnny "Did you say *cave?* Because we—" But before Johnny could say anything else, Bubba stomped on his foot. "Ow! Geez, Bubba! What the heck was that for?"

Roger looked confused. "I'm sorry, Johnny. What were you saying?"

But before Johnny could respond, Nellie was already standing up and extending her hand to Roger. "Well, we've bothered you long enough, Mr. Appletree. Thank you so much for your help. Really, thank you!"

"Yeah...thanks!" said Bubba as he grabbed Johnny's arm and pulled him out the door after Nellie. Logan flashed an awkward smile, nodded, and then followed after his friends.

"Uh...sure. My pleasure. Come back again!" Roger called out, still confused, as he watched the kids run out the door.

Nellie and the boys could hardly contain themselves as they fled the historical society and jumped onto their bikes.

"Did you hear that?" said Johnny. "A cave! He hid it in a cave! Do you think he might be talking about—"

"Our cave?" Bubba jumped in. "Yeah, Einstein. I think it's a good possibility. I mean, how many other caves do you know of around here?"

Logan agreed. "Yeah! And we know it was frequented by Native Americans when they lived in the area. Remember that time we found that old arrowhead in there?"

Nellie was excited too, but she didn't want to jump to conclusions. "I guess he could've been talking about our cave. Who knows? There used to be a bunch of old caves and mine shafts around here until they started covering them up for safety reasons." The boys' excitement visibly dimmed as they considered this. "Then again," she added, "there's only one way to find out!"

That's all Nellie needed to say. Without another word the four of them turned toward the woods and pedaled hard. And as they did, a plain white van slowly pulled out from behind the historical society and began to follow.

12.

It didn't take long to reach the cave, which was just down a hidden side trail along Gypsy Glen Road. Although it wasn't completely unknown in the town—it was a favorite spot for teenagers to come and drink beer and smoke cigarettes—for the most part the cave was left alone. First of all, it wasn't visible from the road. And besides, the poison ivy, jagger bushes, and occasional critter were enough to keep most people from stumbling upon it by chance. This isolation was the main reason Nellie and the boys had chosen it as their meeting spot in the first place.

The four of them had been in the cave dozens of times before, but as they entered it this time they were looking at it with new eyes, paying close attention to every little detail in the hopes of seeing something, anything that might lead them to the amulet.

Nellie reached into her backpack and pulled out the new LED flashlight she'd gotten for Christmas. "Look for signs of digging," she said as she slowly scanned the ground.

Johnny huffed and kicked the dirt floor. "You'd think we'd've noticed something before if someone had buried something in here."

"Yeah," agreed Bubba. "And even if Mr. Appletree did bury it here, he didn't say how long ago. What if someone else already found it?"

Logan wasn't as pessimistic. "Personally I think if someone had found an ancient emerald amulet we'd have heard about it. In a small town like this, something like that would be big news."

"Unless they decided to keep it a secret and sell it," replied Bubba.

Nellie was too focused on searching to do any speculating. "All we can do is look," she said. "Maybe it's here, maybe it isn't. I don't know. But we gotta search every square inch of this cave until we're certain."

Over the next hour or so, Nellie and the boys

scoured the cave but came up empty.

"That's it," said Bubba, emerging from a narrow passage in one corner of the cavern. "I'm done looking. If the amulet was ever here, it definitely isn't anymore."

Johnny agreed. "Yeah. I'm bushed. And thirsty. Anyone wanna go upstreet and grab a pop?"

Nellie, however, wasn't ready to quit. "C'mon, you guys! We can't give up yet! It has to be here. It just has to be! Right, Logan?"

Logan sat down on the large stone that they'd always used as their table during meetings. "I'm not so sure, Nellie. I mean, we don't even know for sure if this is the same cave Mr. Appletree was talking about. The Delaware had villages all throughout this region and even into Ohio. Heck, he could've been talking about a whole 'nother cave in some other state. Besides, I kinda think maybe we should just leave the amulet alone, wherever it is."

Nellie couldn't believe her ears. "Leave it alone? Are you crazy? Something like the amulet...I mean, it's probably the most important artifact in our town's history. It shouldn't just be buried in the dirt, in some dark, damp cave. It should be in a museum!"

"Wait a minute," said Bubba. "I thought we were trying to keep it from those *History Hunters* guys. You ask me, you can't find a safer place than inside some old cave that hardly anyone knows about."

Nellie went to respond but couldn't think of anything to say. Maybe they were right. Maybe the stone was better off buried and lost to history.

"Of course," said Logan, "if we did find it, I guess we could always keep it as our little secret."

"I sure would like to see it and hold it just once," added Johnny. "I never held anything magic before, unless you count my big sister's Magic 8 Ball."

"You're such a dork," said Bubba, as he reached out and gave Johnny a playful shove. It was just enough to throw Johnny off balance and send him falling into Logan's lap. The two of them then went rolling off the back of the big stone, which rocked and nearly tipped over on top of them before falling off to the other side.

"Geez, Bubba!" cried Johnny. "You OK, Logan?"

Logan brushed himself off as he sat up. "Yeah, I'm fine. Filthy, thanks to Bubba. But fine."

"Oops," replied Bubba, smiling. "My bad."

"You guys—look!" said Nellie, pointing to the piece of ground now exposed by the toppled stone. There, in the dim light of the cave, was the unmistakable top of a small metal cigar box flush with the ground around it. As the others moved in for a closer look, Bubba pulled out his lucky pen knife and began to dig the box out of the hard-packed dirt. Once he had the box free, he set it on top of the large stone, as all four of them gathered around.

"Well," said Nellie, her eyes wide, "what are you waiting for? Go ahead—open it!"

Bubba smiled and reached down to undo the latch on the front of the box. Then, slowly, he lifted the lid. Even in the dimness of the cave, the green light from the amulet shone brightly and reflected off the stone surfaces. It was stunning! A true piece of art. Shaped like a spearhead and around three inches long, the stone sat within a hand-carved wooden frame attached to a long leather cord.

Nellie moved in for a closer look. "I...I can't believe it. We found it. We really found it!"

"Unbelievable," said Logan.

"So cool!" added Johnny.

"I wonder how much it's worth," said Bubba, as the others turned to look at him. "What? It's a perfectly normal question. Not that I'd ever consider selling it or anything."

"It's beautiful," said Nellie. "Now I understand why it's so sacred to Roger and his people. Maybe he's right. Maybe it should be left undisturbed. I mean, if this thing fell into the wrong hands, it could—"

"Bring in a hefty little sum, that's for sure."

The sound of a man's gruff voice caught the kids off guard as they spun around to see a dark silhouette in the opening of the cave. The figure then stepped inside, and once again Nellie and the boys couldn't believe their eyes. It was him—the Gas Man!

13.

"You!" exclaimed Nellie. "How...what are you doing here?" Then, angrily, "What do you want?"

A fiendish grin stretched across the man's face. "Oh," he said, "I think you know exactly what I want." He glanced down at the box sitting on the big stone.

Bubba quickly closed the lid and pulled the box close to his chest. "Well, if you think you're getting this stone, you're crazy."

The man began to chuckle. "That's real cute, kid. But here's the thing about me: I always get what I want." He reached down and pushed his jacket aside, revealing the handgun tucked into his waistband.

Logan gasped. "Please, mister," he began, "we

don't want any trouble."

"Yeah," added Johnny. "I mean, we're all big fans of your show and—"

"I don't care about some stupid show," said the man, bending down and stepping further into the cave. "I've got people willing to pay a lot of cash for that little rock of yours. So how about you just hand it over?"

Logan was visibly frightened. "Just give it to him, Bubba! He's got a gun!"

Johnny agreed. "Yeah! It's not worth getting shot over!"

But Bubba wasn't swayed. "He's not gonna shoot us, you idiots—we're kids. He's just trying to scare us."

The smile faded on the man's face as he reached down and slowly pulled the gun out of his waistband. "I wouldn't be so sure, kid," he said. "If I were you, I'd listen to your friends." He took another step toward Bubba and the box.

Meanwhile Nellie had inched toward Bubba and was now right next to him. She had also managed to grab a rock without the man noticing. Bubba turned to meet eyes with her before turning back to the man, who was slowly moving closer. In that brief glance, Nellie and Bubba had read each other's mind. Then, just as the man took another step forward, Bubba set the plan in motion.

"Now!" he yelled. Nellie fired her rock at the man, just missing her target. But it was enough to cause him to stumble backward and hit his head on the cave ceiling. Bubba then tossed the box to Nellie and charged at the man, knocking the gun from his hand and sending him to the ground.

"Go!" Bubba yelled. "RUN!"

The man grabbed Bubba by his shirt and threw him hard against the cave wall, knocking him unconscious. Meanwhile, with the amulet box tucked under her arm like a football, Nellie darted out of the cave, her cross-country instincts sending her bounding down the trail like a deer.

The man scrambled around the darkened floor of the cave, looking for his weapon. Logan spotted it laying on the ground just a few feet away and went into action. Picking up the gun, he quickly shoved it into a dark crack in the cave's wall.

The man looked up just in time to see his gun disappear forever. "No! You little jerk! I'll be back for you!" Then he turned and ran out the mouth of the cave in pursuit of Nellie and the stone.

Johnny ran over to Bubba, who was slowly coming out of his daze. "Oh my gosh, Bubba! Are you OK?"

Bubba sat up slowly, visibly shaken, but unhurt. "Yeah, I'm fine. Logan...where's your phone? We gotta call the cops...gotta help Nellie..."

But as Logan located and picked up his phone from the ground, he noticed the screen was completely cracked. "Crap. Must've broke when you fell on top of me. You got yours, Johnny?"

Johnny shook his head. "Left it on the charger at home."

"Dangit!" Bubba stood up, brushing off the dirt. "C'mon, you guys—we gotta help Nellie!"

And with that the three boys took off running out of the cave to try to help their friend before it was too late.

Nellie took off down the narrow trail that led away from the cave and toward the road, the box holding the amulet tucked beneath her arm. Adrenaline surged through her veins, pushing her faster than she'd ever run before. If she could only get to the road and flag someone down, maybe a passing police car—anyone who could get her and the stone to safety.

But then it hit her: even if she did find help, what would she tell them? That she had a magical amulet and was running from a gun-wielding gas man? They'd think she was crazy. And what about the amulet? The whole point was to keep it safe. If anyone found out about it, who's to say they wouldn't try to keep it themselves or maybe even give it to the *History Hunters?*

Then she thought of Mr. Vincent. *He'll know what to do!* Nellie turned around and began back toward the cave. Then she left the trail and headed through the thick undergrowth and down the hill toward the creek, which she could follow right to Mr. Vincent's backyard. Hopefully he'd be there and know what to do.

The man emerged from the cave and took off down the trail. Reaching the road, he looked all around but the girl and the box were nowhere to be seen. *A car must've picked her up,* he thought. She hadn't been that far ahead of him.

Then, just behind him off in the woods, he heard what sounded like footfalls and breaking branches. *Could be a deer,* he thought. *But it could be the girl.* Retracing his steps, the man went back down the trail, listening closely for sounds as he scanned the forest floor. Off to the right he saw what looked like freshly snapped branches. Looking down, he could see the plants had been recently stepped on. "Bad move, Little Red Riding Hood," he said aloud, reaching down to pull a large hunting knife from a sheath around his calf. "The Big Bad Wolf is on your trail." And with that he set off in pursuit of his prey.

14.

Bubba, Logan, and Johnny slowly emerged from the cave, not sure which way the Gas Man had gone. They wanted to help Nellie, but they also knew they were no match for a full-grown man—and a desperate one, at that.

"You see him anywhere?" asked Logan, crouching to look down the trail.

Bubba shook his head. "No. That dude was movin'. He probably reached the road already."

"Oh man," said Johnny, "I hope Nellie got away."

"Yeah. Me too."

"Well, c'mon!" said Logan. "We can't just stand here—we gotta get some help!" He and Johnny started off quickly down the trail.

But Bubba didn't move. "Wait a second!" he

called out. "There's no way we're going to catch either one of them. And even if we did, that guy'd kill us."

Johnny stopped and turned around. "So what are we supposed to do? Wait here and let him catch her?"

"Nellie's super fast," replied Bubba, "and she got a good start on that guy. I doubt he'll be able to catch her, at least for a while."

"But we can't just sit here and do nothing!" said Logan.

"I know what to do," said Bubba, turning away from the cave and stepping onto a small game trail leading down into the hollow. "C'mon...follow me!"

Johnny and Logan shrugged at each other and then followed their friend. "Where are we going?" shouted Johnny.

"To Mr. Vincent's house!" replied Bubba, bounding down the narrow path. "I know a shortcut through the woods. Hope you guys aren't allergic to poison ivy!"

"Oh, great," said Johnny, doing his best to keep up with Logan and Bubba as he brushed the jagger bushes aside and ran down the trail.

Nellie ran down the wooded hillside, leaping over fallen logs and ducking beneath branches, every now and then pausing to look back for her pursuer. So far, it looked like she had eluded him. Mr. Vincent's house wasn't far off now. Just down the creek a bit and past Devil's Rock. Looking down at the metal box in her hand, Nellie smiled and took off down the hill again.

Meanwhile, on the other side of the ravine, Bubba and the boys rambled down the game trail that led down the hill toward Mr. Vincent's. "Hurry up, you guys! Geez, my grandma can run faster than that!"

Logan huffed and puffed as he tried to navigate the low-hanging branches and root-riddled ground. "It's a little hard to run fast, Bubba, when you got jaggers poking out your eyes the whole time!"

"Yeah," said Johnny. "And Nellie's the runner, remember. Personally, I don't like to run unless something's chasing me. Like a bear."

"There it is!" Bubba yelled.

"What?" cried Johnny. "A bear?"

"No! Devil's Rock!" Bubba pointed at the huge, glacial stone sitting at the bottom of the ravine. "Mr. Vincent's backyard is just around the other side. C'mon!"

Further back up the hill, the man tried to keep his eyes peeled for the girl's trail as he pushed his way through the thick and unforgiving underbrush. He knew his buyer was willing to pay up for the ancient stone, and there was no way he was going to miss out on his big payday, even if it meant he had to take desperate measures.

Suddenly he heard a branch break and what was clearly the sound of footfalls just over the next rise. Sprinting to the edge, he looked down and saw the girl making her way through the underbrush. "Now I got you," he said to himself as he continued his pursuit.

As Nellie approached Devil's Rock, she froze in her tracks. Just across the way she spotted another figure moving through the trees. She dropped to the ground to hide herself, praying it wasn't the Gas Man. But as the figure came out into the open, she sighed in relief as she realized it was just Bubba, followed closely by Logan and Johnny. *Thank goodness,* she thought, happy to see that they were all safe.

But just as she went to call out to her friends, a loud crack from behind made her spin around. Nellie jumped as not ten feet away a large doe turned and bolted away from her through the underbrush. *Whew!* she thought, her heart pounding in her chest. *Just a deer.*

Suddenly a large hand clamped over her mouth from behind.

"Keep quiet," whispered the Gas Man, pulling Nellie down to the ground to make sure they weren't spotted by the boys. "Make one little peep and I'll snap your neck like a twig, got it?"

Then, after the boys were safely out of sight, he spun Nellie around and took the metal box from her hands. "All right, sweetheart, let's go," he said, pointing back up the hill. "And don't try anything stupid," he said, pulling out his knife, "or I might just have to use this."

15.

Nellie sat trembling on the big stone inside the cave, trying not to cry. But it was no use. She was terrified, and she was all alone.

"Yeah, I got the stone," the Gas Man said into his phone as he stood by the mouth of the cave. "But we have a little problem here. Four little problems, actually."

Nellie had no idea who the man was speaking to, but she knew her time was running out. There was no way he was going to let her go, not after everything that had happened. She knew too much.

"Hey! Don't blame me!" the man barked into his phone. "I did what you hired me for. I got the stone, didn't I? It's your mess now—you can clean it up!" He turned and scowled at Nellie. "Just get here. And don't forget the money!" And with that he hung up the phone.

Nellie's mind raced as the man came back into the cave. She knew she had to try something if she was ever going to get out of this. "Look," she said, "why don't you just let me go? I mean, you can keep the stupid stone, if it's that important to you. I won't say anything to anyone—I promise!"

Then man chuckled. "What do you take me for, kid? An idiot?" He took a seat on the old stump that Logan always used, setting the box on his lap. "Just sit there and keep quiet. We'll deal with you soon enough."

As the man slowly opened the box, a fiendish smile grew across his face. Even in the dimness of the cave, the brilliant green of the amulet cast a haunting light on the surrounding stone walls. "Incredible," the man said softly to himself, captivated by the ancient talisman.

Meanwhile, back at Mr. Vincent's house, the old teacher was in his den reading when the boys came bursting in through the back door. "Mr. Vincent! Mr. Vincent!" they all yelled in unison.

"Whoa!" replied their teacher. "Where's the fire? I swear you kids are always in a hurry."

Logan was still trying to catch his breath. "It's...it's him," he said. "We found it...the amulet! We were in the cave...and then he came in with a gun...Keanu Reeves...but then Bubba threw a rock and Nellie got away...and we ran through the woods and—"

"Wait, wait, wait," Mr. Vincent broke in. "First off, who had a gun? Keanu Reeves? You mean the man from the gas company? And I'm sorry if I misheard you, but did you say you found the amulet?"

"The guy we saw in Bubba's basement!" replied Johnny. "He's not really a gas man, though—he's one of those *History Hunter* dudes—and they're gonna steal the stone!"

"Well," said Mr. Vincent, "now I'm completely lost."

"Look, Mr. Vincent," began Bubba, "we went to see Roger...I mean, Mr. Appletree, about the stone, and he let it slip that he had buried it inside the old Gypsy Glen cave."

"Ah! The old Delaware cave!" said Mr. Vincent, smiling. "I should've known that's where he hid it. Good ol' Roger, always the romantic."

Bubba continued. "Yeah, well, we found it underneath this big stone right in the center of the cave, and right then he came in—Keanu Reeves, you know, the Gas Man—and he had a gun!"

"Yeah," Johnny broke in, "but Bubba rushed him and he dropped the gun, and then Logan shoved it down a crack in the wall. And when they were wrestling on the ground, Nellie grabbed the box with the stone and ran out of the cave!"

Mr. Vincent was visibly stunned. "That's certainly an amazing story," he said. "I'm just glad you all are OK. But where's Nellie now?"

"That's just it—we don't know," said Bubba. "After she took off out the cave, the man went chasing after her, and that's the last we saw of her."

That was all Mr. Vincent needed to hear. Picking up the receiver of the old tabletop phone on his desk, he quickly dialed 9-1-1. "Yes, hello, this is Jim Vincent over on Galey Boulevard. We've got a situation over here. Please send someone quick!"

While the Gas Man sat nearby, still entranced by the stone, Nellie decided she'd have to make a break for it. She had no other choice. It was now or never. If she could only get past the man without him grabbing her, she knew she could outrun him on the trail.

But just as she went to make her move, the opening of the cave was darkened by an approaching figure. Nellie couldn't believe her eyes. "You!" she said. "I should've known it was you! You...you creep!"

"Come now," said Rick Jenson, as he stepped inside the cave. "Surely you can think of something better than that, Nellie. It is Nellie, isn't it?"

Nellie was shocked. "How do you know my name?"

"Oh, we know all about you and your little friends—Logan, Johnny, and, what's the other one? Oh, yes—Bubba. What a lovely name. We've been watching you all for some time now. And now, thanks to you, we've found what we were looking for."

Nellie couldn't fight back the tears any longer. "You'll never get away with this, you...you jerk!" she screamed, now sobbing. "We're gonna tell the cops all about you, and then you can kiss that stone and your stupid TV show goodbye!"

Rick Jenson laughed. "Is that so? Well now,

aren't you the feisty one, for someone in your... let's just say, unenviable predicament."

Something about the way he said that last part sent a chill down Nellie's spine. He was right. This was bad. How was she supposed to get out of this one? She was no match for two men. And now her only route of escape was blocked.

Or was it? Although the main part of the cave consisted of this one larger room, Nellie knew there were a few smaller passages further inside that led deeper into the hillside. She and the boys had shone their flashlights down them before, but they had always been too chicken to explore them. But now, what other choice did she have?

Meanwhile, Rick turned to the man, who was still hypnotized by the stone. "Is that it—the amulet?" But the man didn't move. "Hey!" Rick yelled. "I'm talking to you! The stone...let me have it." With that the man snapped out of his trance and stood up, handing over the box and its contents. As Rick opened the lid, the green light of the amulet reflected off his made-for-TV face. "My god," he said, his eyes growing wide. "It's beautiful! The most beautiful thing I've ever seen! It must be worth, I don't know—"

"Millions," said the Gas Man, still looking entranced.

"Yeah," Rick echoed. "Millions." He shook his head to try to break the spell of the ancient stone now in his possession. "What are you still doing here?" he said, turning to the man. "Go and get those other kids!"

"What are we going to do with them? They already know too much."

"We'll figure that out later. Just go!"

The man scowled and looked over at Nellie. "One of those little brats shoved my gun down a crack."

Rick sighed. "Here," he said, reaching inside his jacket to pull out a small pistol, which he then tossed to the man. "And don't mess this up!"

With that the man turned and took off out of the cave.

Things were really getting desperate now, and Nellie knew just what she had to do. "You'll never get away with this," she said. "My friends are at my teacher's house right now, and the cops are probably already on their way." Although she wasn't sure she believed this herself. The last thing her friends knew she had taken off into the woods with the amulet. How would they know she had been caught and taken back to the cave?

"Oh, I'm not worried about you or your little friends," Rick responded, setting the box with the amulet down on the big stone. "Who do you think the cops are gonna believe? A highly respected and internationally known TV star... or a bunch of snot-nosed brats with absolutely no proof?"

Just then Rick's phone buzzed and he pulled it from his pocket to check it. This was Nellie's last chance and she knew it. As Rick turned around to the mouth of the cave, for a split second taking his eyes off of her, she made a break for the box. Rick spun around but only in time to see the now-empty box hitting the ground and Nellie turning to run deeper into the cave as she pulled the amulet and its leather cord over her head.

"NO!" Rick yelled, dropping his phone and running after her. But Nellie was too quick for him. Heading straight for a small opening way in the back of the cave, she squeezed herself through, knowing there was no way her pursuer could follow. Rick reached the opening just as Nellie disappeared deeper into the cave. He thrust his hand inside to grab her, but she was already too far in. All he could do was watch the soft green glow of the amulet fade away as both it and Nellie disappeared into the darkness.

16.

Mr. Vincent hung up the phone. "OK," he said, "the police are on their way."

"But what about Nellie?" asked Johnny. "We gotta find her before Keanu Reeves does!"

"Right!" said Bubba. "C'mon—let's go!" He and the other two boys headed toward the door.

"Now wait a second, boys! Look, I'm just as worried about Nellie as you are. But the best thing to do right now is to sit here and wait for the authorities."

Suddenly the squeak of the screen door in the other room caught their attention.

"Geez, that was quick," said Logan, thinking it was the police.

But just then the Gas Man, all scratched up

and filthy, stepped around the corner and into the room. And he was holding a gun.

"It's him!" said Bubba, as he and the other boys quickly moved around the desk to get behind their teacher.

The man had bloody scrapes all over his face and hands, and his boots were covered in mud. He looked like he'd been wrestling with a bobcat. It made him seem all the more desperate and frightening.

"Who are you?" demanded Mr. Vincent, looking down at the weapon in the stranger's hand. "And what do you want?"

"I'll do the talking, old man."

The teacher focused on the gun. "Look," he said, "there's no need for violence."

"And there won't be, as long as you all do what I say."

Mr. Vincent huffed. "You're bluffing."

"Oh, I wouldn't be so sure about that." The man took a step toward Mr. Vincent's desk.

Johnny was terrified. But something stirred inside him, and he couldn't just stand there and hide behind Mr. Vincent. "The stone is ours!" he said, stepping out from behind his teacher. "You have no right to it! It belongs in McIntosh!"

"Johnny, please," said Mr. Vincent, trying to hold him back. "This isn't a game."

"Good advice," replied the man. "I'd listen to the old man if I were you."

"He's not old!" said Logan, also stepping out from behind his teacher.

"Yeah!" Bubba chimed in. "What he said!"

The man was beginning to grow impatient. "Enough!" He raised the gun and pointed it at Mr. Vincent. "Now let's go, before you make me use this thing."

"C'mon, boys. Everything will be OK." Keeping the boys behind him, Mr. Vincent moved out from behind the desk and began to follow the man, who was slowly backing out of the room. But before they could take another step, the sound of Mr. Vincent's squeaky screen door startled the man. He turned and waited, his gun at the ready.

Suddenly Roger Appletree appeared from around the bend, his trusty cane in hand. Seeing the man with the gun, Roger stopped in the entryway. But instead of appearing shocked, he simply smiled. "Well, it looks like I've been missing all the excitement," he said, blocking the only way out of the room.

The man wasn't amused. "Out of my way, Gandalf."

"Oh that's rich," said Roger. "Not just a criminal, but a comedian, too."

"You'd better do what he says, Roger," said Mr. Vincent. "This guy means business."

"I'm not worried," Roger replied. "I would like to have my amulet back, though."

"Your amulet?" said the man. "Ha! Get out of my way before I lose my patience." The man moved in closer, raising the weapon to Roger's head.

"Mr. Appletree!" screamed Logan.

Now the man was right in front of Roger, the barrel of the gun barely an inch from his face. "This is your last chance," he hissed. "Move or die."

Once again the silence was broken by the sound of the squeaky screen door, and then a loud voice roared through the side window.

"Police! Drop the weapon!" Like something out of a movie, suddenly there were police officers outside of every window, their weapons all trained on the man with the gun.

"DROP...THE...WEAPON!" said an officer appearing slowly from behind Roger.

The man was too stunned to react. He just froze and dropped his gun to the floor as the police swarmed into the room.

"Shame," said Roger, smiling. "Didn't your mother ever tell you that violence is never the answer?" Meanwhile, the officers cuffed the man and pushed him out of the room.

"You kids all right?" asked one of the officers.

Bubba poked his head out from behind Mr. Vincent. "Us?" he said, coming out of hiding. "Heck yeah! We're fine."

"Oh, sure," Johnny chimed in, "like you weren't crapping your pants like the rest of us."

"You would know," Bubba fired back.

"There he goes again," said Logan. "Always taking the high road."

"What about the girl?" said the officer. "Is she here too?"

"Oh my!" said Mr. Vincent. "Nellie! In all the excitement I forgot... C'mon! We have to find her!"

Nellie pushed through the darkness, the cave's cold, damp walls scraping her body as she squeezed through the narrow passageway.

She and the boys had never explored this part of the cave before. It had always seemed too narrow, too scary to traverse. But now she had no other choice.

Pausing to listen, she could no longer hear Rick's curses echoing through the cave. But she couldn't risk going back, not without knowing if the Gas Man would return. She had to keep pressing forward and try to find another way out, if there was one.

Eventually the passageway began to widen and Nellie could hear the faint sound of water trickling somewhere off deeper in the cave. She took a deep breath and leaned against the hard rock wall. She had never experienced this level of darkness before. It was terrifying. Who knew what type of spiders and other nasty little bugs were all around her? Not to mention bats! She'd been terrified of bats ever since one got into her house one night and woke her up, flapping around the ceiling of her bedroom. She could still remember how silly her dad looked—a mesh trash can over his head, a tennis racquet in his hand—as he tried to swat the flying rodent out of the sky. Eventually her mother just opened the window and the critter flew off into the night. The memory made her laugh, and then cry. She wanted to be safe and warm at home instead of all alone in this cold, dark, lonely cave. She began to sob, slowly sliding down the wall to the cave's cold dirt floor.

As the tears rolled down her cheeks, Nellie began to feel something. A warmness on her chest, like one of those things you put inside your boots during the winter to keep your feet warm. The feeling slowly intensified. Then it happened— the amulet began to glow! Its green light grew brighter and brighter, slowly pushing away the darkness and illuminating the surrounding cave walls. Nellie couldn't believe what was happening. As the amulet grew more and more brilliant, the more at peace she felt. It was as if she was no longer alone.

Within seconds the complete darkness had given way, and now Nellie could see that she was in a wide, spacious cavern. She picked herself off the floor and began to look around. All over the walls were strange drawings of animals—deer, wolves, cougars, and beavers. There were also strange but beautiful symbols and other images that appeared to be humans with spears, bows and arrows, and even fishing nets. What looked like a river wound its way throughout the pictograph, moving through forests and mountains. Nellie knew this place—it was McIntosh! Her home. Long, long ago. And it was beautiful.

Then she saw it. Following the path of the river, at the far side of the picture, clear as day was a large arrow with beautiful painted feathers. It was pointing directly at a huge boulder in the room that appeared to be holding up the entire stone ceiling above. Nellie walked toward the rock, and when she did the green light of the amulet revealed a hidden passageway just on the other side. Normally she would never want to go even deeper into the cave, but something inside her told her it was OK. She turned to take one last look at the pictograph before following the soft green light of the amulet down the passageway and into the unknown.

17.

Mr. Vincent and the boys went back up Gypsy Glen Road in the back of a squad car along with two of the police officers. But when they made their way back down the trail to the cave, they found it empty. After a search of the surrounding woods, all the way back down to Devil's Rock, there was still no sign of Nellie.

"This is bad," said Logan. "We should've heard something from her by now."

Johnny agreed. "Yeah. What if something... happened to her?"

Bubba tried to stay cool as usual. "Relax," he said. "I'm sure Nellie's fine. Heck, she's probably back at her house right now polishing the amulet." But deep down he too was worried.

Mr. Vincent approached the boys after speaking privately with the police officers. "Well, there's nothing we can do now but wait and let the officers do their job," he said. "They questioned that man with the gun, but he's not saying anything." The teacher could see the look of concern on his students' faces. "Look, I'm sure Nellie will turn up somewhere and she'll be just fine. Don't you boys worry." But the look on Mr. Vincent's face wasn't convincing anyone.

Just then one of the officers got a call on his radio. "Ten-four," he said. "We're on our way. C'mon boys! Jump in!"

"What's up?" asked Logan. "Where we goin'?"

"Down to the Fort Brodhead site," said the officer. "Some kind of trouble down there."

The amulet glowed just brightly enough to illuminate the tunnel a few feet in every direction. Beyond that was utter darkness. Nellie stepped, carefully, feeling the walls of the narrow passageway as she went. She was frightened of the unknown ahead, unsure if some type of creature lay hidden in the blackness of the cave. Every few steps she turned back to see if anything or anyone was following her, but it was just too dark to see. All she could do was keep moving forward and hope that it would eventually lead to a way out.

The faint sound of rushing water grew louder with every step she took. As the noise intensified, so did Nellie's feeling of claustrophobia, causing her breathing to become short and quick as she navigated through the dim light of the cave. She noticed the ground beneath her feet had begun to slope downward, first just slightly, but gradually more and more. She tried to press against the walls of the passageway to keep her balance, but her feet began to slip on the loose, gravelly floor. Worse yet, with every step she took down the passageway and away from the pictograph room, Nellie noticed the light of the amulet was dimming more and more.

"No!" she cried aloud, shaking the necklace. "Don't go out!" But eventually it did go out, and Nellie found herself once again in complete darkness. Trying not to panic, she kept moving forward, using the walls to guide her way as the roar of unseen water drowned out all other sounds. But as she went to take another step, the ground beneath her foot seemingly disappeared, and she screamed as she went falling forward into the darkness.

The next thing Nellie felt was the icy shock of water as she fell into a fast-moving underground stream. Coming up from beneath the surface, she gasped for air as the rushing water propelled her through the darkness. Even if she could somehow manage to grab onto the walls of the cave, which were whooshing past, there was no-where for her to go. The stream completely filled the surface of the tunnel as it jostled and pulled her along to who-knows-where. All she could do was try to keep her head above water as she en-dured sudden and terrifying drops followed by one hairpin turn after another.

And then, way up ahead in the distance, she saw it—light! At first it was only a pinprick. But as the water pulled her along, the light began to grow bigger and brighter. Approaching the light at an incredible rate, she was glad to be coming out of the darkness but terrified of what lay be-yond that opening. But she was moving too fast to do anything about it.

Fifty feet...thirty feet...ten feet...and then—

WHOOSH!—Nellie went flying out of the tunnel and into midair as the water dropped off below her. The light blinded her. All she knew was that she was falling...falling...and then—SPLASH!—she again struck water and went under. Feeling her feet hit solid ground, she pushed off and swam back up to the surface.

Nellie coughed up water as she doggie-paddled over to the shore, trying to catch her breath. Looking up, she couldn't believe what she saw. She was standing in the Ohio River just below Buttermilk Falls, a popular swimming and fishing spot. Over to the right, two boys with fishing poles were staring at her, their mouths agape.

"That...was...awesome!" said one of the boys, turning back to look the twenty-five feet or so up to the top of the falls.

"Are you OK?" the other one called out.

Nellie looked down to see the amulet still safely around her neck. "Yeah," she said, smiling. "I'm fine." Then, not wasting another moment, she came out of the water, ran past the boys, and took off up the trail that led to town and the site of Fort Brodhead.

18.

"What do you mean we're heading out?" The *History Hunters* production manager couldn't believe what he was hearing. "We still have a lot of filming to do here, Rick. Tear down and pack up? Why?

"Because I said so, that's why," Rick Jenson replied in an uncharacteristically harsh and agitated tone. "This is a wild goose chase anyway, and I don't want to waste any more time or money on it."

"A wild goose chase? What are you talking about, Rick? Since when has that—"

"Did you hear me? I said pack up—NOW! Is that understood?" Rick stomped away toward his trailer, leaving the bewildered production manager in his wake. He had almost reached the door of the trailer, when he heard her cry out.

"Hey, you! Rick Jenson! Looking for this?"

Rick whipped his head around to see a young girl, dripping wet, standing at the edge of the bluff that overlooked the river. She had just crested the hill where the trail led down to Buttermilk Falls. As she started to walk toward them, the amulet still around her neck, everyone in the *History Hunters* crew, including a dozen or so extras who were hoping to get on TV, all turned to look at her.

Rick stood frozen, holding the trailer door handle. Now everyone turned to look at him, waiting for his response. Who was this girl? Why was she all wet? And what was that brilliant green stone hanging around her neck?

Nellie stopped right in front of Rick. "I told you you wouldn't get away with it, you thief! This amulet belongs here, with us—in McIntosh!"

Rick noticed that everyone was now staring at him. He had to think quickly. "I'm sorry, sweetheart, I'm not giving any autographs right now. But if you'll come back some other time, I'd be—"

"I don't want your stupid autograph, you... you...fake! You liar!"

Rick began to scramble. Things were quickly spinning out of control. "Look, little girl," he said, "I don't know who you are or what you're doing here, but this is a live production set. We're filming a TV show here, so I'm afraid you'll have to leave."

Nellie took another step closer to the TV host. All eyes were on her now. "I'm afraid not, *Rick,*" she said, turning around to address the crowd. "This man tried to steal this amulet, this treasure, from us so that he could sell it for a bunch of money! But me and my friends figured out his plan, and he sent his own personal thug after us. Isn't that right, Rick?"

An audible gasp rolled across the old fort site.

"What?" Rick replied, trying to appear shocked at Nellie's accusation. "I would never... Why, you little liar! I've never seen this girl before in my life. And now you're trespassing." He turned to a uniformed man standing nearby. "Security! Would you please escort this little girl off the set?"

By this time, however, one of the bystanders had called the police. Rick noticed a cruiser pulling up across the street, and he wasn't about to stick around. But as he started toward his shiny red Jaguar, he was blocked by some of his own crew. "What are you doing? Get out of my way!"

"What about what this little girl is saying, Rick?" said one of the crew.

And another, "Yeah, is she telling the truth?"

Now more people in the crowd started getting involved.

"Let's just wait and let the cops sort this out!"

"Yeah! Who's this guy think he is, anyway?"

Now desperate to escape, Rick began to push his way through the crowd, but they wouldn't give way. As a scuffle broke out, the police officer called for backup and then made his way over to the crowd, who quickly filled him in on the situation. Now there was nowhere for Rick to run.

By the time Mr. Vincent and the boys arrived a few minutes later, several officers were on the scene and both Rick and Nellie were being questioned over by the Fort Brodhead monument. The boys all ran over to her.

"Nellie!" yelled Johnny. "You're OK!"

Nellie was thrilled to see her friends. "Hey, guys! I'm fine. Just gimme a second." Then she turned to address the police officer, who was signaling for the boys to stay back. "It's OK, officer.

They're with me, and they can back up everything I said."

"You can't do this to me! I'm Rick Jenson!" Mr. Vincent, Nellie, and the boys all turned to see Rick being pressed up against the fort monument and then handcuffed by one of the officers before he was quickly whisked away to a nearby squad car.

"Whoa!" said Bubba. "What are they doing with pretty boy Rick?"

Nellie smiled as she watched the officers put him into the squad car and shut the door. "Oh, nothing much. Just taking him to jail."

"No way!" said Logan.

"Way!" replied Nellie. "He was gonna steal the amulet and sell it. Can you believe that? And, oh yeah, then he was going to have the Gas Man — that Keanu Reeves wannabe — 'take care of us' so we couldn't tell anyone."

"Wow!" Johnny exclaimed. "That's crazy."

Mr. Vincent put his hand on Nellie's shoulder. "That's some story. Are you sure you're OK?"

"Yeah, Mr. V. Thanks. I'm fine."

"I don't get it," said Bubba. "Why are you all wet?"

Nellie smiled. "Now *that's* a story! And I can't wait to tell you all about it."

19.

"Well," said Mr. Vincent, "it seems like everything's back to normal now." It was a week or so after all the excitement, and they were all gathered for a barbecue at their teacher's house, along with Roger Appletree.

Nellie smiled, relieved that all the craziness was over and that she and the boys were all safe and sound. But she was still a little flustered about the whole situation. "I still don't get it, Mr. Appletree," she said. "How did you know? And how did the police..."

"It was really just good fortune, Nellie," he said. "I was on my way over to see Jim when I spotted that filthy man snooping around the house. And when I saw he was holding a gun...

well, that's all I needed to see. I immediately dialed 9-1-1."

"So, let me get this straight," said Logan. "You saw him, you knew he had a gun, and you still came inside. Wow. Talk about brave."

Roger smiled, slightly embarrassed. "Well, the dispatcher told me the cops were already en route. It's easy to be brave, Logan, when you know the cavalry is on its way."

"Wait," said Johnny, "the cavalry? Are you saying those policemen came on horseback? I didn't know that. Cool!"

Bubba sighed. "Dude, you're such a moron."

Johnny shrugged. "What? The cavalry rides horses, don't they?"

Rick Jenson's trial, and that of the so-called Gas Man, turned out to be a bigger sensation than any episode of *History Hunters*. Rick got charged with a number of crimes—turns out this wasn't the first time he'd used the show for his own personal gain—and both of them ended up getting sent away for a long, long time.

As for the show itself, it ended up getting canceled altogether, which was just fine with Nellie. After what she learned about Rick Jen-

son, *History Hunters* just seemed to lose its lus-
ter. Besides, she was more concerned about the
fate of the stone.

"I'm sorry about digging up the amulet," she
told Roger. "We just wanted to make sure those
History Hunters guys didn't find it. Like I said, it
really belongs to McIntosh."

"Oh, that's OK," replied Roger, adding with a
wink, "I guess I didn't do that great of a job of
hiding it after all." Opening the lid of the box in
his lap, he looked down at the beautiful green
stone. "And you're right about it belonging to the
town, Nellie. I have to admit, burying it that way
was pretty selfish of me. I just wanted to make
sure it would be safe. I'm sure we could find a
prominent and permanent place for it down at
the museum."

"Actually," replied Nellie, "I think I might have
an even better place for it. Somewhere where it
will always be safe."

The next day after school, Nellie went back
to the cave, the amulet tucked safely inside her
backpack. Once inside, she squeezed back down
the narrow passageway and made her way to the

secret pictograph room she'd discovered during her escape. She hadn't told anyone about the room, other than the boys, Mr. Vincent, and Mr. Appletree. She knew she could trust them. The way she saw it, the room and its stunning artwork had remained hidden and preserved for so long, it just didn't seem right to let it turn into just another tourist trap. Besides, it was the perfect place to keep the amulet safe and a part of McIntosh forever.

A couple weeks later, as a safety precaution, the town covered the opening of the cave with some large boulders and a few tons of dirt. And with that, the amulet was once again a part of history.

But that was just fine with Nellie. Something told her that Pisquetomen would've wanted it that way.

ACKNOWLEDGMENTS

Special thanks to Linda M. Au, Carrie Cernetic,
Hugh Harper, Jackie Jaros, Sara Jones,
Mike Kelley, Corey Olszanski, James A. Perkins,
and of course, my wife Cassie.

The Real History
Behind the Story

The Secret of the Amulet is, of course, a work of fiction. However, as in most works of fiction, there are little nuggets of truth sprinkled throughout.

When I first started thinking about this story, many moons ago, I knew I wanted it to take place in a small town much like my hometown of Beaver, Pennsylvania. I also wanted to pay tribute to my town's rich heritage and give some much-deserved attention to Pisquetomen—yep, he's real—whose Delaware brothers, Shingas and Tamaqua (aka King Beaver), have always gotten top billing around these parts. Pisquetomen never actually had a magical amulet, at least not to my knowledge. But he did serve as a guide and translator for Moravian missionary Christian Frederick Post (1710–1785) during his diplomatic mission to gain the favor of the Ohio Indians during the French and Indian War.

I decided to call the town "McIntosh" because that was one of the names the town of Beaver went by before it officially became a borough in 1802. That's because before there was ever a town here, there was Fort McIntosh (1778–1788). This lonely old frontier fort, named for Lachlan McIntosh (1725–1806), stood high up on a bluff overlooking the Ohio River. Built during the American Revolutionary War, it was meant to serve as the first in a series of stepping-stone forts that would support an attack on the British stronghold in Detroit. Although that plan never fully came to fruition, the fort did help provide some security to local settlers. It was also the site of the Fort McIntosh Treaty of 1785, which ultimately led to the Ohio territory being opened to peaceful settlement. For this story I chose the name Fort Brodhead after Col. Daniel Brodhead (1736-1809), who replaced Lachlan McIntosh as the commander of the Continental Army's Western Department during the Revolutionary War.

"Old White Eye" is based on a real person, too. And contrary to this story, he and Pisquetomen definitely were not the same person. Koquethaqechton (1730–1778), aka White Eyes, was chief of the village of Coshocton (Ohio). He pushed for peaceful coexistence with the white settlers, as long as his people could still have their own land and governance. Unfortunately, he may very well have been murdered by the Americans who were wary of his growing influence.

And, oh yeah, History Hunters is what I call the local history club I run in my hometown.

Some other little nods to my local area:

- **Buttermilk Falls,** located in nearby Homewood, is one of my family's favorite places to have a picnic and do a little hiking. Unfortunately there's no secret tunnel behind it (at least not that I know of).
- **Bug Park** is what we used to call my local park—Bouquet Park—when I was a kid, because some of the playground equipment resembled giant insects.
- Other real places mentioned in the story: **Gypsy Glen Road, Galey Boulevard, Devil's Rock, Scotty's News, Two Mile Run, Witch Flavor,** and **Don's Deli**.

Thanks for reading!

Photo by Richard Kelly (richardkelly.com)

About the Author

Valentine J. Brkich is a writer from the small town of Beaver, Pa. When he's not writing, he enjoys hanging out with his family, eating french fries, reading about Bigfoot, and napping. (Not necessarily in that order.)

His other works include:

- *Achieving Mediocrity: Surefire Strategies for a Lackluster Life*
- *The Chronicles of BoogieFace and The Animal: One Small-Town Dad's Adventures in Fatherhood*
- *Cageball, Poker, and the Atomic Wedgie: And other tales of Catholic school mischief*
- *Bridgewater: A Narrative History of a Pennsylvania River Town*
- *Get Yourself An Inflatable Baby Sitter: And other survival tips for first-time dads* (ebook)

Web: ValentineBrkich.com
Instagram: @smalltowndad
Twitter: @valentinebrkich

www.ingramcontent.com/pod-product-compliance
Lightning Source LLC
Chambersburg PA
CBHW021205130626
46554CB00005B/2000